WHISPERS OF GUILT

A DCI JAMES CRAIG NOVEL

JOHN CARSON

DCI James Craig series
Ice Into Ashes
One of the Broken
Dead on Arrival
Whispers of Guilt

DCI HARRY MCNEIL SERIES

Return to Evil
Sticks and Stones
Back to Life
Dead Before You Die
Hour of Need
Blood and Tears
Devil to Pay
Point of no Return
Rush to Judgement
Against the Clock
Fall from Grace
Crash and Burn
Dead and Buried
All or Nothing
Never go Home
Famous Last Words
Do Unto Others
Twist of Fate
Now or Never
Blunt Force Trauma

CALVIN STEWART SERIES
Final Warning
Hard Case

DCI SEAN BRACKEN SERIES

Starvation Lake

Think Twice

Crossing Over

Life Extinct

Over Kill

DI FRANK MILLER SERIES
Crash Point
Silent Marker
Rain Town
Watch Me Bleed
Broken Wheels
Sudden Death
Under the Knife
Trial and Error
Warning Sign
Cut Throat
Blood from a Stone
Time of Death
Old School - short story

Frank Miller Crime Series – Books 1-3 – Box set
Frank Miller Crime Series - Books 4-6 - Box set

MAX DOYLE SERIES
Final Steps
Code Red
The October Project

SCOTT MARSHALL SERIES

Old Habits

WHISPERS OF GUILT

Copyright © 2024
John Carson

www.johncarsonauthor.com

John Carson has asserted his right under the Copyright, Designs and Patents Act 1988, to be identified as the author of this work.

This is a work of fiction. Names, characters, places, brands, media, and incidents are either the products of the author's imagination or are used fictitiously. Any resemblance to actual events, locales, or persons, living or dead, is coincidental.

Without limiting the rights under copyright reserved above, no part of this publication may be reproduced, stored in or introduced into a retrieval system, or transmitted, in any form, or by any means (electronic, mechanical, photocopying, recording, or otherwise) without the prior written permission of the author of this book. Innocence is and

All rights reserved

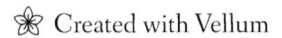

❃ Created with Vellum

ONE

As a forensic pathologist, Annie Keller was used to cutting open dead bodies, but she couldn't handle them at this stage of their life, where they were nearing the end of the road. That took a special kind of person.

Like Garfield Clover, one of the nurses who looked after her uncle.

'Got a fag, Annie?' he asked her as she strode down the corridor towards him.

'A fag? Are you daft? I gave up smoking a while back.'

He stopped when he reached her. 'Aw, c'mon. Just one. I'm begging you.'

'You know there are such places as newsagents

and supermarkets, places where you can go in and hand over some money, and in return they'll give you a whole packet, just for yourself.'

They started walking down the corridor together, dodging other nurses, and some old people who were out for a stroll, heading to the TV room or...wherever.

'I lost mine. The one I keep in my pocket as a reminder of what a bad bastard I once was,' Garfield said.

'Smoking isn't a sin, Garfield.'

The man was tall and wide, with red hair. All he needed to do now was grow whiskers and lick his arse and he'd be the spitting image of the cartoon cat.

'Why don't you get a pack and keep it in your pocket like me?' Annie said.

'I'd smoke them. I don't have your willpower. But if there was just one, then I'd think, wow, I just have one left, so I can't smoke it.'

'That certainly is willpower. It's what I do. Although I've fallen off the bandwagon now and again, and I only have five left,' Annie said.

They turned right, heading towards her uncle's room.

'Was his nibs in again?' Annie asked.

'Which one? His drunken old pal or the snooty son?'

'The son.'

'Wait a minute, I can't quite remember. It must be the lack of tobacco in my pocket. Maybe if I had a fag, I'd be able to remember more clearly.'

'Oh for God's sake. That's extortion. I know somebody who would lock you up for ten years for that.' She tutted and pulled out her packet of cigarettes, which was battered and looked like she'd just fished it out of a rubbish bin. She popped one out and handed it over.

'Oh, lovely,' Garfield said, smiling at his new-found treasure. 'That's very kind of you.'

'Bugger off, kind. That's theft, that is. Same as.' She put the packet away.

'You're a sweetheart.' He grinned at her. 'If I didn't have a girlfriend, I'd be setting my sights on you.'

'Phhh. Like you could attain this.' She swept her hands up and down in front of herself.

'Stranger things, and all that.'

'So spill; was my esteemed cousin Martin here earlier?'

Garfield rolled his eyes. 'He was. And a royal

pain in the arse he was. Again. My dad needs water. My dad needs food. My dad needs this. My dad needs that. Jesus, I almost told him what *he* needs, and that involves some leather being inserted into a crevice that never gets any vitamin C.'

'Just the usual, then?' Annie said.

'The man's impossible. His father has stage four dementia. Touching stage six.' Garfield stopped at William Keller's room. 'He's been talking funny lately. Since you were last here.'

'I was only here a week ago,' Annie said.

'I know that, but it started the day after.'

'Talking funny, how?' she asked. 'Like a pirate or something?'

Garfield looked at her. 'If only. No, he's started talking gibberish, and also as if there's somebody in the room with him who only he can see. Just thought I'd give you a heads-up.'

'Thanks, Garfield. Maybe my cousin talking about the cases that he presides over sent the old man over the edge.'

'Okay, m'dear. Thanks for the fag. I'll see you before you leave.' He winked at her before moving away, and Annie went into her uncle's room.

William Keller, once a judge, now a shadow of

his former self, was sitting in a chair next to his bed. His eyes went wide when he saw her.

'Come in, quick,' he said, waving her over. He leaned forward in the chair, looking from side to side as if there might be somebody hiding under the bed or waiting to jump out of his closet.

'How are you doing, Uncle Bill?' Annie said. She had known her father's brother all her life and remembered the good times they'd had when she was growing up. She was fond of him – unlike how she felt towards his son. Martin was a judge like his father had been, but Annie thought the man was sterner, and she couldn't remember ever seeing him smile. This was probably the reason he was a confirmed bachelor.

'Never mind how I'm doing,' her uncle said. 'You need to pay attention to what I'm going to say. I might be dead tomorrow.'

'Don't talk like that, Bill.' She always started off with *Uncle Bill*, then transitioned to just *Bill*, because it was easier.

'Bollocks. Just listen; there's a killer in here.'

It took all of Annie's willpower not to roll her eyes and admonish him. He was obviously harking back to his working days, when he'd seen his fair share of murderers.

'I think they're all just retired people like you, Bill. I don't think there are any killers in here.'

He looked at her then, and she was amazed at how sharp his eyes were.

'He's in here. I know he is. I've seen him.'

She locked eyes with Bill then. 'I'm sure it was somebody who maybe looked –'

'Albert Fish,' Bill said. 'That's his name.'

'Listen, Bill –' she started to say, but he smiled at her and cut her off again.

'I heard that Hannah Copeland passed away. Nice woman. We often stopped in the high street for a cup of coffee. I miss that. She wasn't well, you know.' He put a hand up to the side of his mouth and whispered, 'Cancer. Lady parts.'

Annie nodded her head. 'That's a shame.' Hannah Copeland had died ten years ago, and she remembered that her uncle had been upset at the time. The poor woman had died of ovarian cancer.

'Why don't we get you a nice cup of tea?' she suggested to Bill. 'I brought some of those fancy wee cakes that you like.' *You know, the ones that will block your arteries and kill you, but at your stage of the game, that's the least of your worries.*

'Aye, that would be nice, Alice. Maybe you could

call Martin and have him come round for a nice cuppa. I haven't seen him in a long time.'

Alice had been known to Annie as Auntie Alice, Bill's wife. She'd been dead for the past five years. Annie didn't tell Bill that his son had already been in. His mind had switched from killers roaming the halls of the nursing home to being back home with his wife.

'Let's get wired into these cakes,' she said, bringing the box out.

'Smashing. I love these cakes. But shouldn't we wait for Alice?'

'She said to start without her. She'll be along shortly.'

'Well, if she doesn't get her skates on, they'll all be gone.'

He took one of the small tarts with a cherry on top and bit into it. He ate in silence, while Annie just watched. She didn't have an appetite for the cakes and would leave them with Garfield to dish out to the old man.

Annie felt sad, knowing that the dementia would eventually take her uncle away and there was nothing anybody could do about it.

'Did you see him?' Bill asked.
'See who?'

He looked at her like she was daft. 'Fish, of course!' A darkness had moved into his eyes now.

She was about to ask whether he meant the singer, Derek Dick, but thought better of it. 'No, Bill, I didn't see him.'

She usually humoured him when they were having their fantastical conversations, but she just couldn't feed into this killer idea.

'Well, he was here. And he's the reason Stephen Colby is in the asylum.'

'Who's Stephen Colby?' Annie asked.

Bill looked at her again, confusion on his face. 'Who?'

Annie shook her head. 'Never mind.'

They sat and chatted about random topics before Annie said her goodbyes.

Out in the hallway, Garfield had one hand in his tunic pocket.

'That you off, sweetheart?' he said to her.

'I am. Take care of your fag.'

'I'm going outside on my break and I'm going to smoke the arse off it,' Garfield said, grinning.

'You said you wanted to keep it like a lucky charm.'

'I also said I can cook, swim and dance the fandango.'

'I knew that was all horse shit,' Annie said.

'And yet you still love me.'

'Always, Garfield, always.'

'As I said, if I wasn't attached, you and I –'

Annie held up a hand. 'Let's leave some mystery. Some things are not meant to be spoken.' She laughed and walked away.

TWO

DCI James Craig stood looking out of his living room window, at the bridges over the Forth in the distance. The view never failed to move him.

Now the house was officially all his. After his wife had decided that their separation was official and they were headed for divorce two years down the line, he had bought her out with his share of the proceeds from the London home they had sold and what was left in the bank.

Eve Craig had quit the school district in Fife and had moved into a little house near the State Hospital, where their son was incarcerated. He didn't know what she was doing for a living and he didn't care.

He scrunched up the letter from his solicitor that

he was holding and tossed it on the floor. At once, his German Shepherd shot over to it, thinking this might be a ball.

'No, Finn, it's just a piece of shite.'

He was holding a tumbler of whisky and he drank some, feeling the burning in his gut. It felt good.

The dog barked at him, wanting Craig to go and get a ball now he had teased him with something that was a fake.

'In a minute, boy. Go eat your dinner. Annie will be here shortly.'

He sat down and the dog lay down beside him, deciding to rip up another of his toys. Craig didn't mind; it was better than listening to him bark.

Heather, the woman who came in to look after the dog during the day, was also a writer. Just starting out, she could kill two birds with one stone. She had suggested that he start writing. She was sure he had a mountain of stories inside his head that he could put onto the screen and sell on Amazon. He had sat and thought about when he worked in the Met in London, and thought that maybe he could squeeze a few ideas into books. Basing his fiction on some real-life stories. Others had done it, so why couldn't he?

He saw Annie's Audi pulling up outside, so he left the living room and went through to the kitchen. The house design was inverted, so that the entrance and the bedrooms were downstairs, and the other rooms were on this upper level, to give the residents a better view over the bay.

He poured her a glass of wine and heard the front door being opened. Finn stood with his ears up, looking around. Craig wasn't sure if the dog was still expecting Eve to walk through the door, but he would be just as pleased to see Annie. When he had answered her earlier text, he'd told her he'd leave the door unlocked. He wasn't exactly dating her, but they had been spending a lot of time with each other. She mostly stayed over at his place rather than him staying at hers, because of the dog. But it wasn't every night.

'It's me!' she shouted from the front door, and the dog took off, barking, taking his ball with him.

He heard her laughing and the dog barking. At least he hoped that was the order of things.

Then Finn came up first, turning to drop his ball at the top of the stairs.

'Finn! For God's sake, give Annie a chance. At least I think it's Annie. Maybe it's my six o'clock appointment with the travelling masseur.'

'You wish,' Annie said, reaching the top of the stairs. She picked up the ball and threw it gently for the dog, missing a vase and Craig's tumbler, which he had put on the coffee table. She walked out of the living room and went into the kitchen.

'How's my favourite detective?' she said, walking over to him and putting her arms around him. She kissed him gently on the lips.

'I don't know, but when I see him, I'll tell him you're asking for him.'

'Don't be sad; you're a close second.'

He handed her the glass of wine he'd poured. 'How did the visit go?'

She sipped some of the wine and sighed. 'He's gone over the edge. He thinks there's a killer roaming the halls of the home.'

'Oh Jesus.'

He led her through to the living room, where they sat on the couch, Finn lying down on his dog blanket.

'He told me there's a killer called Albert Fish in there.'

'Is he still on medication?' Craig asked. He picked up his tumbler and sipped his drink.

'Yes, he gets it every day. But today he seemed different. Usually, he's all over the place, but there was a break in the clouds for a moment and a little sunbeam popped through. Like there was a light in his eyes that isn't there normally. It was weird.'

The doorbell rang, and Finn was up and barking and running down the stairs to scare off whoever was at the door. Craig hoped it was the Chinese he'd ordered before Annie got there, and not some Jehovah's Witness.

It was the takeaway order, and Craig assured the young man that Finn was friendly. *Just don't do anything stupid.* The young guy had been to the house before, but still he had that look that certain people give German Shepherds, some of the time because they'd been in trouble with the law.

'Thanks, son,' Craig said, closing the door on the delivery guy, and told Finn to get upstairs. The dog obliged and ran ahead.

Then Craig remembered the letter from his solicitor. Twenty-five years of marriage down the toilet. More years if you counted the ones when he and Eve had been seeing each other. He had known then that she was the one for him and he didn't want anybody else. But after they'd found out their son was a serial killer, things had shifted in their marriage.

When Joe had been moved from the psychiatric

hospital in Edinburgh down to the State Hospital in Carstairs, that had been the writing on the wall. Eve wanted to be near Joe, and she'd jacked her job in and asked him if he too would move down there.

'And do what?' he had asked her. 'Be a school lollipop man?' They had gone back and forth on that one, him arguing that she could drive down to see Joe, her arguing that she wanted to be close in case anything happened. They reached an impasse, and neither of them budged. She had gone down to live there, and he had thought she would get it out of her system, but she hadn't. Joe was her son, and she could look past what he had done. Craig was on the fence about that. The last six months or so had been hellish, and although he didn't think he could just switch off his feelings for her, the bright light that had once shone was now more like a little candle flame.

He had slept with Annie after feeling a connection with her, and now he thought there might be something there other than just a quick rebound fling.

Upstairs, the dog was standing looking at a ball, barking for Annie to kick it to him.

'Finn, that's enough,' he said, going through to

the kitchen with the food. The dog followed him, with Annie bringing up the rear.

'It's my turn to buy the food,' she said to him.

'It's okay,' he said, smiling.

'Wait a minute,' she said, 'why would I let you buy me dinner, then ply me with drink, then drive me home, invite yourself in for a nightcap, then take me upstairs and make love to me all night? Why would I do that?' She cocked her head at him.

'Because I drive a Ferrari?'

'Smooth-talking bastard.' She laughed and put her arms around his waist. Then she stepped back and gently slapped his arm. 'You never said you had a Ferrari.'

'It's a little model one. It's on the bookcase in the living room.'

'You need to get your line of patter sorted out, Jimmy-boy. Or else you might start thinking my head's zipped up the back.'

'I'm a bit rusty. Maybe I should go clubbing more often.'

'You can if you like. We're not attached at the hip.'

'I might break a hip if I go dancing,' he said, starting to open the food containers.

She laughed and looked at him. 'I mean it; we're

friends, but we're not married. You're free to do whatever you like now.'

He smiled at her. 'Don't worry, I'm not having a midlife crisis. I won't buy a sports car and go dating a young woman.'

They sat on the couch and ate at the coffee table, watching TV. It was less formal than the dining room.

'How's work?' he asked her after they'd finished and he'd cleared the plates away. The dog made a brave attempt to lick the plates, but Craig didn't encourage him.

'So busy,' Annie said. 'We're at capacity right now. I'm knackered, but I have to go on.'

'We should think about maybe going away for a weekend,' he suggested.

'What do you have in mind? New York?'

'Maybe just York.'

'Last of the big spenders. But maybe we could go to Amsterdam?'

'They seem to be getting pissed off with tourists at the moment,' Craig said.

'Well, just wait until they have none and their economy is down the toilet. See what they say then. I say they can shove it.'

Craig laughed. 'We can think of something. But this weekend is the big bash, so that's out.'

'Ugh. Tomorrow I turn forty-five. What happened to my thirties?'

'Some people don't make it to their forties. I'm just thankful I wake up in the morning.'

'Trust you to get all philosophical on me.' She smiled at him.

'You want some more wine?' he asked her.

'Before I answer, am I driving home or staying here tonight? I really don't want to wake up on my own on my birthday. Not this year. Last year I had a cupcake with one candle on it.'

'If that's what madam wants, madam will be received with great pleasure,' Craig answered.

'I bet you say that to all the girls.'

'Only the ones who want to stay overnight.'

He disappeared and brought back the bottles of wine and whisky, and topped up their glasses.

'Cheers,' Annie said.

Craig pulled his laptop out of its bag and sat it on the coffee table, powering it on. 'Let's have a search for this killer your uncle mentioned.'

He signed in, Annie looking away. Not that he minded, as he could have changed the password, but she looked away anyway.

'Albert Fish?' he asked her. She turned back towards him and nodded.

'It sounded like a weird name,' she said.

'It's a real name,' Craig said.

They looked at the photos of a man, clearly taken a very long time ago. He was wearing what looked like a bowler hat, and he had a moustache. The photos were in black and white.

Annie put her glass down on the table and looked closely at the laptop screen. 'Look, it says he died in January nineteen thirty-six. In Sing Sing, the American prison.'

'He was a real bad bastard by all accounts,' Craig said. He opened the Wikipedia page and read more about Fish. The man had killed a child, for which he had been put in the electric chair.

'My uncle's getting worse, Jimmy. I know there's going to be a day when he doesn't recognise me anymore. He's getting more and more like that every time I see him.'

'It's sad, I know.'

'He also mentioned somebody called Stephen Colby. Is that a name you're familiar with?'

Craig shook his head. 'It means nothing to me. Let me google the name.'

He typed in Colby's name and up came newspaper articles from thirty years ago.

'It says here that Colby was a serial killer. He got caught thirty years ago. He slipped through the cracks at first. The police caught him, but the court let him go. He had been done for assault and he got off. But then a tip-off led the police to his house, and they found all sorts of trophies in his attic. They charged him with killing six women, but they reckoned he killed a lot more.'

'Jesus. Was my uncle Bill the judge in his case?' Annie asked.

Craig scanned the story before looking at her. 'Yes.'

'He obviously remembered the name.'

'You'll never guess what else,' Craig said.

'You're switching to Ys because boxers just aren't cutting it anymore?'

He grinned at her. 'That was the next piece of news. But no; Colby is incarcerated at the State Hospital. With Joe.'

'Holy cow. His defence must have gone down the road of, *Our client couldn't possibly have killed those women and be of sound mind.*'

'Looks like it. You want to read about this guy?'

'Absolutely.'

Craig handed over his laptop, and Annie sat with it on her lap while Craig got up to go to the kitchen to make coffee. Finn got up, doing his shepherding duties.

Craig brought through the coffees, and spent some time on his phone, checking texts.

'This Colby is a piece of work,' Annie said. 'He brutally tortured those women and denied everything, even though they found a box of trophies in his house. Jesus.'

'Maybe I'll go and talk to him tomorrow,' Craig said. 'It would be interesting to speak to him face to face. See if he remembers Bill.'

'I'm sure he does. He's the judge who put him in that hospital.'

After browsing the internet some more, they sat and watched a DVD, some romantic thing that bored Craig, but he watched it because Annie wanted to watch it.

'I got a letter from my solicitor today,' he told her. 'The separation is official. Eve's staying down in Carnwath. She wants to be near Joe.'

Annie sat up. 'How do you feel about that?'

'It is what it is. I mean, I'm not going to pretend it doesn't sting a bit, but that's what she's chosen.'

'I want to say I'm sorry, but if things had stayed

the same with you and Eve, I wouldn't have got to know you better.' She put an arm through his and pulled him closer and kissed him.

'There's always a silver lining.'

She smiled. 'Let's go to bed.'

'It's early.'

'I don't want to sleep. And it's my birthday tomorrow.'

THREE

Annie Keller had woken up feeling happy and sad at the same time. She'd been happy that Jimmy Craig was lying beside her – and Finn had climbed up to be beside them during the night – but sad that she was forty-five and not happily married. Her ex-husband couldn't keep it in his pants and had been sleeping around. Him being a surgeon, it was easy for him to transfer to Edinburgh, where he now lived.

Where would this relationship with Craig go? She wasn't sure, but she knew she hadn't felt this happy in a long time. Cuddling a hot water bottle while watching a chick flick could only stretch so far.

Now, she was riding down in the lift to the mortuary, where she was starting to have a little backlog of bodies. Victoria Hospital was also starting to reach capacity, so they would soon have to send any suspicious deaths over to Edinburgh, which wasn't unheard of.

She heard chatter coming from her office as she went past the entrance doors. Two new mortuary assistants had been hired: one of them had been a lab technician – Seth Cameron, a nice young guy with hair that looked like he had stuck his finger into an electrical socket; and Drew Harrison, a slightly older man who had transferred from Dundee.

'Morning, boss,' Seth said, finishing his cup of coffee.

'Morning,' Drew said.

'Good morning, gentlemen,' Annie said, slipping her lightweight jacket off. 'What delight awaits us this morning, do you think?' She knew who was first in line to ride the *Annie Keller Y-Incision*.

She hung her jacket on the coat stand in the corner. Then she stopped suddenly, seeing the little wrapped box on her desk. She held her breath for a moment; it brought back memories of the stalker she'd had for a couple of weeks, a man who had turned to murder and who was now being held in Edinburgh's Saughton prison.

'One of the nurses brought that down,' Seth said. 'Cat from Ward Four.'

Annie let out her breath. 'Oh, that was nice of her.' She didn't touch it, but would get around to it later.

'If I'd known it was your birthday...' Drew said. He didn't finish the sentence. 'I'll buy the coffees later.'

'Thanks, Drew.'

'I'll spring for some doughnuts,' Seth said, feeling like he had been backed into a corner now and not wanting to look like a cheapskate.

'Again, thanks. I'll take you both up on that. First, though, let's see what our sudden death from yesterday died from.'

'We'll get right on it,' Seth said.

They left her office, and she was just switching her computer on when she sensed a shadow at her door. She let out a little gasp and her head shot up. Ever since she'd had a stalker, she'd made sure scissors were within reach on her desk, and her hand automatically reached out to grab them. But then she saw it was her cousin.

'Christ, Martin, you should cough or something when you come along the corridor like that.'

'God, I'm sorry, Annie. I heard what happened with that bastard who was stalking you. I never thought.'

'No matter. But I don't want to be the one pulling the scissors out of your chest on a steel table, especially if I'm the one who put them there in the first place.'

Martin Keller subconsciously put a hand up to his chest and rubbed it. 'I don't think I like the idea of being stabbed by anything,' he said. 'I imagine you've seen all sorts in here.'

'I've seen some horrific things that human beings have done to other human beings. It makes me think of the sort of punishment that some people deserve and don't get. But that's just me.' Annie remembered having a similar conversation with him at a party one time, knowing that Martin was a judge. Like it was *his* fault that some scum buckets still roamed the earth.

'Luckily, we live in a civilised society.'

'Indeed.' The lack of both alcohol and the willingness to verbally spar with her cousin ended that chapter in the conversation. 'Are you here just to check on my personal safety, or...?'

'No, no, nothing like that. I'm quite sure you can take care of yourself, Annie.'

'Come in and sit down. Coffee?'

'No, thank you.' Martin came in and sat down.

She saw he was wearing casual clothes, not the

usual garb he wore when he was sitting on the bench in Kirkcaldy.

'I can indeed take care of myself,' she said as he moved about in the seat, trying to get comfortable, like she was giving him a warning in case he thought about trying to slap her or something. 'What brings you here, Martin?'

'I have a week off.'

'And this is how you want to spend your time? Or are you just at a loose end?' She smiled at him.

'Going for lunch with a friend today, but I wanted to come and see you first.'

Annie sat back and looked at her cousin. He was ten years older than her, with salt-and-pepper hair, and a face that had seen a lot of bad things in his career but hadn't seen too many fists. He had a look about him, the sort of guy you would think twice about causing trouble with in the pub. He had that air about him, promising you that he would fight back if push came to shove.

He cleared his throat. 'You've been going to see my dad, Garfield said.'

Annie knew the big nurse hadn't been sworn to secrecy. 'Yes, I try and get in a couple of times a month.'

He took in a breath and exhaled slowly. 'I

wanted to ask you: has he been talking even more nonsense than usual?'

'I wouldn't call it nonsense, Martin. He has dementia.'

'No, no, I don't mean nonsense that way. I mean, has he been talking about some killer walking about the hospital?'

Annie didn't want to blurt out, *Yes! He's been talking shite for weeks now*, so instead she answered in an even voice, 'Yes. He thinks there's a killer called Albert Fish in the home. Fish is –'

He held up a hand. 'I know. An American serial killer from the nineteen thirties. God knows what he's been listening to. Maybe some podcast, if he can even comprehend that.'

'Maybe it's in his subconscious. Something he read about years ago, and that little nugget stayed in the part of his brain that isn't filled with fog.'

'I honestly don't know what it is, Annie, but it worries the hell out of me. Is that a sign that he's near the end? God knows I'm aware that he doesn't have a return ticket, but just the thought of him not being in my life anymore scares the bejesus out of me. He was my mentor. He taught me things that no book can teach you, and it helped me be the person I am today.'

'I can't think of him not being here without feeling shock or sadness. I can't imagine Uncle Bill not being in the home anymore. It was hard enough when you had to put him in there.'

'I could have sold his house, but I just can't. I have power of attorney, but selling his house would mean drawing a line under his life. Does that make sense?'

'Of course it does.'

'I just hope when the time comes, he goes quietly.'

'Me too, Martin.'

'Listen, I won't take up any more of your time,' Martin said. 'However, I wanted to ask if it would be alright if I brought along a plus one to your party on Saturday?'

'Of course,' Annie said.

'It's somebody I've known for a long time, and ever since Sarah left, Michelle and I have got to know each other a bit better.'

'That's fine. I look forward to meeting her.'

'I'm sure you'll like her,' Martin said, standing up.

Annie stood and walked round her desk and gave her cousin a hug.

'I'll try and go this weekend to see your dad. I don't want to leave it too long.'

'I appreciate that.'

Annie watched her cousin leave the office and it made her feel more vulnerable. Her own father was in his seventies, but she hadn't spoken to him in years. Not after the bust-up after her mother's funeral. She thought she should maybe mend some fences.

With that thought in mind, she went out to join her two colleagues.

FOUR

'You know something, when you tell a girl you're taking her for a drive in the country, she doesn't expect to end up outside the State Hospital for the criminally insane,' DS Isla McGregor said from the passenger seat of Craig's Volvo.

'How does the inside of the hospital grab you?' Craig said, turning the engine off.

'If they have a machine that dispenses doughnuts, I'll let you off the hook.'

'They have a canteen that serves coffee and foosty rich tea biscuits.'

'Don't worry, boss, I'm sure you'll find us somewhere nice to have lunch.'

'It's barely past breakfast time,' Craig said, looking at her. He wondered how she could put so much food away and still stay slim. She had told him it was her metabolism working like a ship's boiler room. Craig had questioned whether ships had boiler rooms nowadays, or instead had engine rooms. Isla had told him that it was a figure of speech, while her tone had suggested he stop being a smartarse.

They got out into air that felt warm after the chill of Craig's air conditioning. While it wasn't exactly Ibiza weather, where the heat slapped you as you got off the plane, it was a welcome relief. Isla had had to put on the heated seats on the way down. 'Since I apparently have no fat on me,' she had told Craig, giving him the side-eye, suggesting that maybe *he* did. She didn't suggest he dress in shorts and a t-shirt all year round like all the other fat bastards she knew, despite the temptation in her mind yelling at her to go for it.

'Annie seems to be in a chipper mood since you two have been...'

Craig looked at her, waiting for what was coming next, which may or may not be filtered.

'Been what?' he said as they crossed over to the main reception unit.

'Stepping out with each other.'

'What does that even mean?' Craig said. 'It

sounds like something my great-grandmother might have said.'

'You know what it means. Don't start getting all coy with me now. Wenching. Playing the sausage fiddle.'

Craig laughed. 'Christ. You just made that last one up, didn't you?'

'And on the fly too. Not bad, eh? But don't try and use your specialist interrogation tactics on me. Just give me some of the details.'

He stopped and looked at her. 'Like what?'

She grinned. 'Does Finn like her? What's her favourite colour?'

'He does, and you would know that better than me since you've known her a lot longer than I have.'

'It's blue, and don't think you can change the subject. We're not finished. This is just the end of part one,' she said as they stepped up to the door and were buzzed in.

'I'm sorry, but you haven't kept up the payment on your subscription, so you'll no longer be able to access any live streaming. Or any other kind of streaming. That means no more gossip, in case you weren't grasping the analogy.'

'That was a very poor analogy, if you don't mind me saying.'

'I don't mind at all,' Craig said as they showed their warrant cards.

Craig spoke to the receptionist, and they were escorted over to the secure wing, where the patient would be brought to them.

'Seriously, Annie seems a lot happier since you started dating her,' Isla said.

'Now we're being a bit more modern. Using phraseology that my father would have used.'

'Oh, piss off,' Isla said in a low voice.

'Now you're getting down to my age group.'

'This is not over, Jimmy Craig. Annie will tell me everything anyway, since we're besties.'

'Will she?' Craig replied, raising his eyebrows.

Isla was silent for a moment. 'No. But there's nothing stopping you.'

'I don't kiss and tell.'

'We're colleagues, boss. We drink together. I tell you dirty jokes. I'll wash your car.'

'We are. We do. You do. And no thanks.'

The nurse, a big guy who looked like he pulled tree stumps out of the ground in his spare time, escorted them to the room where Stephen Colby would be brought in.

They sat down at a table on chairs that were bolted to the floor. One chair sat opposite, also bolted. The table had been given the same treatment, so if Colby decided to take a benny, then it would be fists and boots all round, although Craig doubted that Colby would be wearing hobnailed or anything else of that nature.

It turned out that he was wearing flip-flops – harder for them to run in if they made it past the fence unattended – and he wasn't exactly shackled when he came in.

Craig was expecting to see a buff guy in his fifties, somebody who had worked out for the past thirty years, but Colby was skinny, with a pair of glasses that made him look like a professor. Not to be underestimated, Craig thought. Sometimes the skinny ones were the most dangerous when you let your guard down.

Two attendants stood by the door that Colby came through, ready to pounce.

'I don't believe we've been introduced,' Colby said.

'I'm DCI James Craig, this is DS Isla McGregor. Thank you for seeing us today.'

'It's not like I have anywhere else to go.' There was no smile on Colby's face, just crow lines by his eyes. His hair was short and he was clean shaven, but it was the piercing eyes that had locked on to Craig's that drew attention. He sat with his hands clasped on the table. 'You're here to talk about Sandra McCallum. My psychiatrist talked to me about it, about dredging up the past. He's worried. I told Dr Ward that there's nothing to worry about. I've been here for thirty years. Time enough to think about the killings over and over.'

'Thirty years to maintain your innocence,' Craig said.

'That's right. And it hasn't changed. Not once. I've been told many times to just come clean, that it will lift a weight from my shoulders. That allowing the families of the missing women to give them a decent burial will cleanse my soul.'

'I'm not here to ask where you buried the bodies,' Craig said.

'That's good, because I wouldn't have an answer for you,' Colby replied. His voice was monotone, bereft of any feeling, and it sounded like a recording that had been played over and over a million times.

'We just want to get your side of the story,' Isla said.

'Why?' Colby asked her.

'Your name came up in conversation,' Craig said. 'It would be interesting to hear your side of things, telling it to two officers who weren't around at the time.'

Colby's eyes flicked between them like he was looking for a catch. 'What's in it for me?' he said.

'Nothing,' Craig said. 'You can go back to your room and do whatever it is you do. Or you can sit here and tell us your side. What do you have to lose?'

'I've told everybody who would listen for the last thirty years that I'm innocent. Okay, I got accused of beating up some guy after being in the pub one night. I didn't hit anybody, but the police didn't want to know. Luckily, the jury saw right through them.'

'Tell us about that night, Stephen. We're interested to know what happened.'

Colby sighed and started to tell his story.

'I had friends back then, quite a few of them, and we'd go out on a Friday night. I had a girlfriend too, and we would sometimes go out in a foursome on a Saturday night, going over to Edinburgh on the train, or we'd stay in Dunfermline, have a meal and a drink. Good times. But the supposed attack happened on a Friday night when I was out with Stan and Gerry. Stan was ginger, so we called him Ginge the Radge. He was off his rocker that boy. Mental. Didn't give a toss about anybody, and would fight his own shadow if he thought it looked at him the wrong way.

'We were out drinking in the pub, the Malt Shovel, waiting until the club off the High Street opened, which was usually about ten. We were fine, not blootered, just having a few pints and a laugh. Then this guy came in, three sheets to the wind, and bumped into me. One of my friends told him to watch where he was going. You know the sort of thing – words that start wars. I just ignored him, but he stopped and turned, and came right up to me. Asked me what my problem was. I told him there was no problem. He looked at me and then went to the bar. He had a few more drinks and then left. We left shortly after that to go to the club. Nothing else happened that night.

'Then the following morning, I got a knock on the door. The police. They arrested me and charged me with assault. Said I'd kicked the shite out of some twat. It turned out it was Martin Keller. His old man, William, was a judge. I mean, Keller couldn't identify me as his attacker, because it wasn't me. But it went to trial and it was found not proven. I walked out a free man.'

Craig looked at the man, getting the feeling he was telling the truth.

'If it wasn't you, Stephen, who do you think did it?' Isla asked him.

Colby locked eyes with her. 'God alone knows. I know it wasn't me, but nobody believed me. And that, my friends, was the least of my problems. After that, they came at me with a vengeance, and it worked.'

'They?' Craig asked.

'Your lot. No disrespect, Jimmy, but I was fitted up. And I realise that you've probably heard that a million times, but this time it's true. I didn't harm any women, never mind kill them. They said I killed at least six women, and that they found trophies from the kills in my attic, all from women who had been reported missing. They were missing because I killed them, according to the police. But there's one fly in their ointment.'

'What would that be?' Craig asked.

'One of them is still alive.'

FIVE

Edinburgh

'Come on, Layla, it's for the greater good,' Arnold Palmer said. He looked around at all the overgrown bushes in Warriston Cemetery and wondered if they would ever make headway in this place.

'I'm just resting,' Layla Hogg replied.

'Arnold Palmer?' a young man said, grinning at him. 'Like the golfer?'

'Shut up.' It was a jibe Arnold had heard all his life.

Norman turned away, laughing. Arnold knew the young man wasn't all there and he made allowances, but being daft only carried so much weight. Norman was Layla's son, and she insisted on bringing him to the weekly meeting of the Warriston Warriors. It was a select group of people who got together to do their bit for the historic last resting place of some very famous people. An eclectic group of people, some retired, others fitting in some bush-whacking when they had the time. Some, no doubt, came along just for the little refreshment afterwards. Arnold himself was partial to a lemonade shandy – with a double nip poured into it – and knew the rest of them enjoyed one too. Even Norman enjoyed pouring money into the puggy, but Arnold had once seen the young man's face change, from a smiling, hopeful light in his eyes to the look of a murderous nutcase, when he ran out of money and had nothing to show for it.

Arnold carried an old leather coin purse in his pocket in case he found himself in the unfortunate position of being alone with Norman behind some out-of-control hogweed. He'd give the bastard some-thing more to think about other than a blister from the hogweed sap. One sap was going to irritate him for an afternoon, while the other would knock the fucker's front teeth out.

'You're such a fusspot, Arnie,' Layla said. Arnold liked it when she called him Arnie. It made him feel like he was big and strong like that guy in the films. Arnold Squirtashaker or something.

Layla was ages with Arnold, retired but not quite over the hill, a woman who liked a tipple and a quick rumble when they could find the peace and quiet. He'd tried his luck the last time they'd had their cemetery outing and she had been enthusiastic, but then, when they had been what Layla would call canoodling on the couch, Norman the fuckwit came in, shouting for his ma, telling her he had been robbed.

Arnold had jumped up, thanking God that his trousers weren't round his ankles.

'What do you mean, robbed?' Layla had shrieked. Her hair could have done with a bit of brushing at the back since Arnold had messed it up, but Dafty didn't notice.

'That bloody puggy is rigged. It took five quid off me! Luckily, I'd bought an orange juice before I invested my money.'

Invested his money. That was what the little bastard called his gambling habit. And now he was swaying a bit on his feet, like orange juice was the last thing he had been drinking. Arnold had watched Layla go into her purse on more than one occasion to find her money short. She thought she was being a bit absent-minded, but Arnold suspected – but couldn't prove – that Norman Bates was doing the dipping.

'Must be strong orange juice, son,' he'd said.

Norman had grinned like an idiot. 'I think the barmaid fancies me,' he replied.

Fancies a fucking axe in her head, more like. 'Oh yeah?' *Blind, is she?*

'Yeah. She's got nice teeth. I think she wants to get married.'

Jesus. 'Well, if you spend more time there, she'll get to know you better.'

Layla had slapped his arm. 'Don't encourage him.'

Arnold looked at her. 'He's got to get out and enjoy himself. Meet new people, you said.'

'I did. That's true. Here, take this, son, and go back and have another couple of lemonades.'

'Orange juice.'

Lemonade, orangeade, who gives a toss? Just bloody well leave. Arnold knew when to keep his mouth shut, though. The thoughts tumbling around inside his head were stopped at the gate before they could get out.

'I think I'm going to be sick,' Norman had said, and put a hand to his mouth.

'Fuck me,' Arnold said, side-stepping the anticipated flow of puke.

'Upstairs, quick!' Layla said.

Norman had turned and run out of the living room, and Arnold heard the thumping of Norman's feet on the stairs, closely followed by Layla's. Then the unmistakable sound of somebody returning the orange juice he had rented for a couple of hours.

Even if Dafty had left after that, even if Layla had come back down wearing nothing but her wrinkly birthday suit, Arnold couldn't have done anything more strenuous than play Scrabble. To say the mood had left would be an understatement. It had not only left but packed its bags, got on the next stage out of Dodge and told him that there was a chance it wasn't returning. Arnold would have to do some serious thinking about whether he was going to try it on with Layla in her house again.

He didn't want to take her to his own house. First of all, he was living with his daughter and her husband. His son-in-law made Norman look like Einstein, and the fat bastard couldn't spell work, never mind find any. But Arnold told himself this was only a short-term arrangement. He would find his own place again. In the meantime, he was trying to put some money away so he could invite Layla away for a weekend in the country. He knew she would only agree to this if she could be convinced that her son wouldn't burn the house down.

Plan B was to ask her to marry him so he could move in with her, and then when the laddie was out doing God knows what, they would have a go on the Arnie-coaster.

'You okay there, Arnold?' a woman said, coming up behind him. He spun around; he was convinced he had seen a ghost in this cemetery one time, and he thought that the apparition had become real.

It was only one of the other team members, Maggie something-or-other. She was not the world's best-looking woman, but she had her attributes, like the fact that she was a widow and was number two on his list of women he wanted to spend time with.

'Maggie. I didn't see you there,' Arnold said, his heart racing like a freight train. He had gently told her before to cough or whistle or make a rustling noise with the stick she carried. Or even shout out that she needed a piss. Just something other than creeping about like she was one of the undead.

'You look a bit frustrated. Everything okay at home?'

He had forgotten what a nosy cow she was. Her ranking in the top ten might slip down a notch or two. Her one redeeming factor was that she knew how to have a good laugh when she was drunk. She swore, told dirty jokes and could be as crude as the guys. While getting disapproving looks from Layla and a woman named Tabitha, the men all thought Maggie was a hoot when she'd downed a couple.

'Everything is just fine, Maggie. The back is giving me a bit of bother today, that's all.'

'Oh, shame. Just take it easy. It'll soon be pub time.'

'And to the Lord we thank it,' Dennis said, coming round a tree. Arnold didn't quite like the man. Creepy old bastard who didn't have much conversation in him other than stories of how things worked or who'd done what in history. He couldn't tell you who was running the country, but he could tell you Napoleon's mother's auntie's maiden name.

Arnold got bored off his tits listening to the man, but couldn't help picturing the old duffer popping his clogs in the pub. Sick, he knew, but it wasn't like they would go raking about in his wallet if that happened. Unless the next round was his, of course, then all bets were off.

'How about we switch it up today?' Dennis said.

'What do you mean?' Arnold said. Maggie stood

looking at him, while Norman stood looking at a stick.

'Let's go somewhere else for a drink.'

'Like where?' Maggie asked, her eyebrows knotted now, as if Dennis had suggested a stripper bar.

'I don't know. Just somewhere different. We could broaden our horizons beyond Goldenacre.' Dennis's false teeth danced a bit, like they too had got excited at the prospect of a new locale, but he reined them in just in time.

'No, thanks,' Maggie said.

'Yeah, I'm with Maggie,' Arnold said. 'I'm quite happy to go to our usual.'

The smile slipped a bit, as if the old-timer could see some Hun coming over an imaginary hill and he was going to have to use his bayonet on the bastard. Arnold saw Dennis gripping his shovel handle a bit harder. He knew it was a bad idea to give the old sod a shovel; he was supposed to take care of hogweed with it, but Arnold and one of the other men had a pool going, betting that Dennis would get confused one day and dig up one of the residents.

'Just a thought,' Dennis said, and turned away, disappearing into grass that was so high, it was doubtful if it could even be called grass now. Arnold thought he could hear mumbling coming from Dennis, calling them a bunch of ungrateful bastards, and fuck them all.

Arnold knew the old sod would be the last in the pub and first out before putting his hand in his pocket.

'I'm having a party next weekend,' Maggie said.

Arnold took a stick of chewing gum out of his pocket, knowing it was the last one. He unwrapped it and popped it into his mouth. Every time he'd asked Maggie if she wanted one, she would say no.

'You want one?' he asked her.

'Oh, go on then.' She held out a hand.

Arnold stared at her. Maybe if he hit her with his shovel, he could bury her and nobody would notice. No, he wasn't built for prison. 'Actually, that was my last piece. I was just being polite. I don't have any more.'

'Why did you ask me then?'

Did you not hear me saying I was just being polite? Dozy cow. 'I don't know.'

'That wasn't very nice.'

'You always refuse.' Arnold chewed his gum noisily.

'You're not getting invited to my party,' she said, walking away.

'And you've just dropped down my list to number nine,' he said quietly.

'What did you say?' Maggie said, turning back to him.

'I said, you really want me there and I'll see you at nine.'

She grinned. 'I can't be angry with you for long, cheeky chops. I'll tell you where I live when we're in the pub.' She walked away and Arnold kept his mouth shut this time.

Layla came crunching through the undergrowth towards him, a machete in one hand. 'What was she saying?' she asked.

Arnold thought that he should tell Layla that it was none of her business, but he also thought he wanted to stay in one piece. 'Dennis wanted to change venues, but Maggie didn't want to. And frankly, neither do I.'

'Somebody should tell Dennis that we're not his army unit.'

'I'll leave that up to you. I'm just working my way up to having a pint.'

'Don't drink too much. Norman's going over to his friend's house this afternoon.'

Arnold looked puzzled. 'Friend? Like a real one? Not the imaginary one who lives in his wardrobe?'

'Nope. You know Norman plays a lot of video games?'

Arnold had thought the man went upstairs to look at boobies on Tik Tok. 'I didn't but go on.'

'He plays on the internet, and he met some other young man who lives with his parents, and he's going round to his house later.'

Don't all grown men who play video games live with their parents?

'That's nice.' Arnold didn't think this was nice at all. He thought that maybe Norman had fallen foul of a group of people who would get him round to an abandoned house so they could roll the daft bastard, but who was he to stop him? Arnold would be alone with Layla.

'I'll stick to just one of my usual shandies. I'll tell the others that I'm on antibiotics.'

'Like that time you had to take them for that rash you got cutting down some weeds in your garden?'

'No, no, nothing like that. And let's not mention that to the others. The words "rash" and "antibiotics" in the one sentence will send their minds into a flurry of lightly veiled gossip.'

'Your secret's safe with me.' Layla put a hand on his arm and giggled like a little girl.

'There's no secret.'

She giggled more and walked away.

'No, really, it was a nettle rash or something.' But it fell on deaf ears. 'Oh, fuck off then. You won't be giggling when I go to Maggie's party and she takes me upstairs with her.'

Maggie popped her head up from behind some tall grass and looked at him.

'Another Maggie,' he said and wondered if he should chop a foot off just to divert her attention.

Just then, Norman came booting through the tall grass. He'd come from the addition, the small part of the cemetery that ran alongside the old railway line.

'I found something,' he said, out of breath.

Arnold let his shoulders slump. 'What is it?' he said. 'Pirate treasure? A ghost?'

'A man,' Norman said.

Arnold wondered for a brief moment if there was some weirdo hanging about in here, and if all the men combined could tackle him. Certainly, Layla might be up for chipping in with her machete. Dennis was probably already reliving some battle, and if they shoved him to the front, maybe his mind would dredge up some long-forgotten fighting skills.

'Where is he?' Arnold asked, then kicked himself. Of course this man was going to be where Norman had just been.

'In there.'

'Is he alive?' Arnold thought to ask.

Norman shook his head.

Aw fuck. Arnold put an arm around Norman's shoulders, not wanting to get too close as the man's bathing habits, according to his mother, were questionable at the very least and downright bogging at the worst.

'This is a cemetery, Norman. There are lots of dead men. But they're underground. They can't harm you.'

'I know that,' Norman said, shrugging him off. 'This one's above ground. Arsehole.'

'Arse–' Arnold started to say, but then Layla came up before he could go full-tilt on the little bastard and give him a piece of his mind.

'What's wrong, pumpkin?' she said.

This nickname was new to Arnold. It was probably one she used with her son when the bastard was having a nightmare and came downstairs in his jammies holding his teddy bear. Last week.

'I saw a man, Mummy.'

Mummy? Arnold bit his tongue. Norman was probably going to have a play date with a serial killer who was going to cut him up and put him through a mincer.

'Where, darling?' Layla shot Arnold a look, suggesting that he should have pampered to Norman's little fantasy. 'He gets spooked sometimes in here if he wanders away on his own.'

'He's forty-five,' Arnold said in his own defence, wondering if the doctor had gripped the tongs just a little bit too hard when they pulled Norman out of his mother's birth canal.

'You know he's fragile.'

Arnold looked at Layla's son, all seventeen stone of him, and thought that maybe he was going to give the serial killer a run for his money after all. 'I do, but don't coddle him.'

'Don't tell me how to treat my son.'

Arnold held up his hands and followed them through the stone archway into the extension, which was in an even more rundown state than the main cemetery. For the life of him, Arnold couldn't see what Norman had been doing in here. Probably standing and thinking how pretty the sky looked.

'Where was he, petal?' Layla said, going into overdrive with the cotton wool.

'He's still there,' Norman said, giving no further indication of where this man / figment of his imagination was.

'Well, he's gone now. So come out and be with us.'

'No, he's not,' Norman said, making a face like he had last Bonfire Night when he'd said one of the guysers was calling him a freak and Layla had told him he was just calling him Frank.

'There's nobody here, Norman.'

'There is! Over there! Near the bushes.' He pointed to the ivy creeping up the wall, and when Layla and Arnold both looked down, they saw some blue material.

Arnold waited for Layla to move forward, and when there was no indication of her taking a step, he gingerly walked over, keeping a tight hold on his shovel in case it was a druggie lying down and shooting up (this was an expression he'd picked up from a cop show), or worse, waiting to ambush them. But when he got closer, he saw the man wasn't of this world anymore, and not in a ghostly way.

Whatever he had looked like at one time, he didn't look like that now.

'I quit this Warriston Warriors shite,' he told Layla. 'You better call the police.'

SIX

Edinburgh

There were enough cold cases in Scotland to keep Police Scotland busy for a very long time. The cold case unit was up to its ears in cases, so when the MIT wasn't working on a live case, they would pitch in.

DCI Harry McNeil's team was no exception. Edinburgh had had its fair share over the years, and the team looked at every angle like the case was brand new. Like they were doing now, as Harry thought about breaking for lunch.

Detective Superintendent Calvin Stewart was in his office, which overlooked the incident room, and they could all hear him shouting at somebody on the phone.

'Christ, I wonder who's getting his jotters now?' DI Charlie Skellett said.

'Has anybody noticed that the DSup is getting a wee bit more touchy these days?' DS Lillian O'Shea said. 'Or is it just me?'

'I think it's just you,' Harry said. 'What say you, Charlie?'

'Aye, I'm not noticing the difference, Lillian. He's always shouting at somebody.'

DC Colin 'Elvis' Presley swung round in his chair to look at them. 'I think he's just the same moaner as he always was.'

'Who's a moaner?' Stewart said, stepping out of his office. Some of them thought he must have oiled the door hinges recently.

'My old man. Moaning old sod,' Elvis said, thinking on his feet.

'You should show respect for your old man, ya wee bastard. You don't know when he's not going to be here.'

'Sorry, sir. I'll take that on board.'

'Good. My daughter always tells me she loves me, and the wee fella, my grandson, tells me the same.'

'I love you, Calvin,' Skellett said.

'Oh, fuck off. You ruined it there, Charlie,' Stewart said.

'I was in the moment.'

Stewart tutted. 'I bet you're one of those fannies who gives the ending of a film away.'

'Behave yourself,' Skellett answered. 'That reminds me, have you ever seen *The Sixth Sense*?'

'Bog off.' Stewart looked at the others. 'Listen up; we got a shout to go to Warriston Cemetery. Apparently, some jungle explorers found what they're saying is a body that looks like it could be poured into a bucket. Their words, not mine. Grab your stuff. Harry? You're in charge.'

'Sir,' Harry said.

'Where's Miller?' Stewart asked.

'In the toilet.'

'Right.'

At that moment, DI Frank Miller walked in and they all looked at him. 'Did I miss something?'

'A shout,' Harry said, getting up out of his chair. 'You and me in one car. The others can fight amongst themselves.'

'You mean I've got to sit in your bogging Mondeo,' Miller said.

'It's only until I get a new one.'

'You said that six months ago,' Miller complained.

'It's not my fault it's still running,' Harry said, grinning.

'Plus he's a tight wad,' Stewart chipped in.

'Right, let's get down to this place before my character is completely assassinated.' Harry turned to Stewart. 'Did the caller say which part of the cemetery the body's in? It's a big place.'

'I told patrol to have a car waiting at the gate. Apparently, they had a hoor of a time finding it, but then a bunch of people wearing last year's ugly Christmas sweaters and anoraks flagged them down.'

'Right. See you down there.'

SEVEN

On the other side of the Firth of Forth, James Craig was drinking a mug of coffee and sitting at a computer when Detective Superintendent Mark Baker walked in. Looking rough as usual.

'How did you get on, Jimmy?' he asked. His shirt looked like it had been slept in and his suit had a new crease that hadn't been there the day before.

'Christ, boss, I thought you were still on Tinder? Finding women and taking care of yourself?'

Baker sat down on an office chair next to Craig and rolled it closer to him. 'This is not as easy as I thought.'

'You told me you'd met somebody.'

'I did. And I had. But it went sideways.'

'Jesus. What happened? Did you suggest you'd take her for something to eat, then buy her a bag of pork scratchings down the boozer?'

'Oh, shut up. I know how to treat a woman. But let me tell you about her. She's thirty.'

Craig's eyebrows jumped up. 'Thirty? Lucky bastard.'

'No, no, wait till I tell you about her. She's thirty and never been married. She was engaged, she told me, a while ago. She's a stunner.'

'Too much for you to handle?' Craig suggested.

'Behave. I'm in my fifties, Jimmy. I've been round the block a few times. I know how to handle women.' Baker looked around theatrically to make sure nobody else was looking. The others were busy at their own computers and weren't near them.

'If she was a stunner, why aren't you still going out with her?' Craig asked.

'I'm getting to that point. Anyway, she tells me she's back in Fife after working down south for a while. She had sold her flat before she moved, and now she's moved in with her widowed mother in Lochore and is looking for her own place again. Physically, she has curves in all the right places, she dresses well, she has a great sense of humour – but as I said, she's never been married.'

'I feel like there's a red flag popping up.'

Baker nodded. 'I thought to myself, how has she not been married? Good-looking girl like that? I found out why she's never been married.' He looked at Craig.

'Am I supposed to guess at this point?' he said in a low voice.

'No, I'll tell you. She's a fucking psycho.'

'Like...a real psycho?' Craig said.

Baker nodded. 'Grade A nut job. We had been out three times, and you know what they say about the third date.' He raised his eyebrows at Craig and nodded his head a few times, like they were about to use a secret handshake. 'With this woman, it was the first, second and third date. She wasn't shy. She told me she had been looking for somebody like me: mature, sophisticated, knows how to treat a woman. I was pleased, let me tell you.'

'I can imagine.' Craig left out the next bit about asking what type of guide dog she had.

'I thought I'd nailed it, if you'll pardon the pun. But then something started to crack. It started one night when we were in a social club, and I shit you not, it was like flicking a switch, watching her whole demeanour change. A woman said something to her, and the smile dropped off her face like a magnet off aluminium. She stood up, grabbed the woman's hair, pulled her face in close and told her if she ever said something like that again, she'd slit her fucking throat. I told her to stop, but she looked at me and told me to back off. It's been a long time since I nearly shat myself, but something cold ran through me that night.'

'You called it quits after that?' Craig asked.

Baker shook his head. 'Oh, trust me, I wanted to, but when we left, the other side of the coin came back. The smile was in place, and she apologised, said she didn't know what had come over her. But I knew that other side of her was the real personality. She was putting on this nice one for me. She begged me to take her back to her mother's place and spend the night.'

'Begged you?'

'Well, not in so many words. But I caved, Jimmy. It's been a while since the wife left me and I have needs. And there's hardly a line of women beating a path to my front door.'

'That's true.'

Baker shook his head. 'Anyway, I spent the night, and then when I woke up the next morning, she wasn't in bed, but I could hear raised voices. She was arguing with her mother, and I heard the old woman telling her that she shouldn't mess this one up, meaning the relationship. That she blew it with her fiancé with her temper, and to keep it under control or I'd never marry her. Marry her, Jimmy! Fuck me, I was only wanting some fun.'

'Then you dumped her?'

'Actually, when I said it went sideways, I meant I'm shitting myself about breaking it off with her. I broached the subject, telling her that maybe it was a mistake, but she begged me not to break it off.'

'You spent the night with her again, didn't you?' Craig said.

'How dare you! Are you suggesting I'm weak and think with my small head?'

'That's exactly what I'm saying,' Craig answered.

'Bastard. You're right. I can't sleep for worrying about what she's going to do when she finds out that I have no intention of marrying her.'

'I don't think you'll have to worry about the small brain; she'll cut it off.'

'Christ, Jimmy, don't be talking like that.'

'You better watch out she doesn't get pregnant.'

Baker sat back as if Craig had slapped him. 'I didn't think about that.'

'You wouldn't have, since you were thinking with the small brain.'

'I'm going to call her now.' Baker looked at Craig. 'Unless you want to call her for me. Tell her I'm deid or something.'

Craig laughed. 'I don't think so.'

'Maybe I'll tell her I've been seconded to Shetland.'

'Listen, boss, just tell her the truth. You've enjoyed her company, but you don't want to lead her down the garden path, and you're not ready to get married. Especially since you're technically still married to your wife.'

'I'm not going to tell her about my wife. She thinks I'm a widower. They're all lying bastards on these dating sites. That was my lie.'

'Do yourself a favour; next time, be upfront with a woman. And maybe get one who's more your age.'

Baker stood up. 'My age? Not bloody likely. Thanks for letting me bounce that off you, though, son.'

DS Dan Stevenson held up a phone. 'We have a shout, sir. There's a body been found on the Fife coastal path.'

Both Baker and Craig looked at him.

'What are the details?' Craig asked. Meaning, what are the specifics? Man, woman, child? Age range?

'This is a weird one. The caller told control that this person is dressed in man's clothes, but he has no face. The caller, a woman, was hysterical. When patrol got there, they called it in to us. The body is badly decomposed.'

EIGHT

Christopher Ward was the best psychiatrist the State Hospital had ever had. By his own admission. Some of the others looked down on him, like the doctors who had been here since dinosaurs roamed the earth. But he didn't give them the time of day. They were from an era when a lobotomy was the answer to everything. Well, not quite, he thought, but not far off it. Some of them had probably been personal friends of Freud himself. One of them, he was sure, had been a personal confidante of Adolf Hitler. Nasty old bastard. Not only did he have a foreign accent bubbling away underneath but a lisp as well. Ward wouldn't have hired him as a custodian never mind a doctor.

But that was neither here nor there. The state

shithole, as some of them called it, was a stepping stone to Ward having his own private practice one day. His clients would have money, and they would give him lots of it to make them feel better. He knew somebody who had his own practice, and he stated from the beginning, when he was first introduced to his clients, that not everybody could afford him. His clients were elite, and his pricing was for them only. His psychology worked on every one of them. Those who had money wanted to part with it just to be part of the little group.

Right now, though, Ward had to make a name for himself in the hospital. Even if it meant suffering that little shit Joe Craig. The serial killer son of that copper. He had actually seen the bastard in here, talking to that other numb-nuts, Stephen I-Never-Touched-Them Colby. Another waste of space. Not one of Ward's assigned patients, so he didn't give a crap.

One thing he *was* interested in was Eve Craig. Ward didn't like to think of himself as a predator, but he did take advantage of certain situations.

Like Christine Thomas. She was such a beautiful woman, but she was married to Henry Thomas, who had been sent to this dump for psych evaluation after he'd battered two men to death with a steel scaffolding pole, then said he couldn't remember doing it.

Ward had clocked the bastard right from the word go. He was faking it, no doubt. But Ward had to evaluate him a few times, ask him all sorts of questions, delve into his background.

Ask him questions about his wife. Sexual questions.

At first, Thomas had asked him why he was asking those sorts of questions, prying into his private affairs, but Ward had sat back and told Thomas to his face that he was facing life in prison for murder unless they could prove he was – *fucking unhinged* – suffering from a mental disorder that had made him commit the crime.

Thomas had zipped it up after that. The big, fat bastard wanted more than anything to be deemed unfit to stand trial. Ward wasn't going to give him a free pass. He put Thomas through the wringer, trying to poke and goad him into have an outburst, so they could have a peek behind the curtains, but to give the man his due, he didn't drop the act.

Ward had requested to have a talk with Christine on a few occasions, and she had readily agreed.

He told her that her husband was indeed insane.

That was his professional opinion and the one he would give to the court.

Christine had cried then. In his office. He had offered her a box of hankies, and she had stood up and put her arms around him, sobbing into his shoulder. He had smelled her perfume then, sucking it in through his nostrils, like he was absorbing her soul. Or some such shite like that. He would remember that line if he had to start writing poetry for her. In the meantime, it just felt good to be in her arms.

She had sat back down and asked him what the future held for her. He told her honestly that if her husband wasn't insane, he'd be put in prison for the rest of his life, but that wasn't going to happen. He'd be committed to this hospital for the rest of his life.

She had told him that Thomas had had outbursts before, that he had a violent streak in him. Ward assured her that he would get the best help in here.

As he got to know her better over the next few months, she began to open up to him more. She invited him over for dinner, and since they both lived in Glasgow, he had readily agreed. He had told him that he could get in trouble for having dinner with her, and she had replied, *What will they do to you for sleeping with me?*

Ward hoped he wouldn't have to find out. He

took advantage of her vulnerability, making her feel safe and secure, and telling her – made up – things her husband was telling him in his sessions. Like when he had beaten his grandmother when he was a teenager, and had fought with his father, and had once stabbed another man in a fight with a screwdriver. Ward didn't want to make up anything about Thomas hurting animals. That was a line he wouldn't cross. He could put up with Thomas driving a bus full of nuns towards a cliff and then jumping out, but he wouldn't hear of anybody hurting an animal.

Christine had been aghast. These were things that she didn't know about her husband. Ward had smiled inwardly; he didn't want Christine visiting Thomas too much, and when she did turn up, he wanted her to feel like she was going to vomit at the sight of him.

Ward had never married. He didn't feel the need to spend a fortune on a woman just to have her move in and take over his happy life. He preferred to have fun with them, and when the fun wore off, call it a day. He spoiled a woman when he was going out with her; he just didn't want to spend the rest of his life with any one of them. He didn't cheat on them either; that wasn't what he was about. He just wanted to play the game.

Christine had been fun. Of course, she had still visited her husband, but as time passed, she became increasingly repulsed, and Ward knew it was time to strike.

He told her that her husband had confessed that he'd almost murdered Christine in her sleep. He had watched her sleeping, listening to the horrendous snoring, and had thought about lifting a pillow and suffocating her with it.

Christine was horrified and told Ward that she didn't even know the man she had been married to. They had made wild love that night.

Two weeks later, Henry Thomas was dead. He had dropped down dead of a heart attack at age thirty-nine. There would be no recommendation that he spend the rest of his life in the State Hospital. He would spend the rest of eternity in a wooden box.

After the funeral, Christine dumped Ward, much to his relief.

Now, he was sitting with Eve Craig in her living room. She had showered and dressed and had made him coffee, which was weak, so he'd just drunk half of it.

'This is a nice flat,' he said, thinking it was a hovel.

'Thank you.'

She walked over to him and kissed him, closing her eyes for a moment, but that only served up an image of her estranged husband. She opened her eyes and kissed Ward harder.

'I'd better get to the hospital. We don't want to be seen arriving together. I'll prepare Joe for your visit.'

'Thank you, Chris.'

He put on his light jacket and left her flat.

NINE

The house was on the main road, and they could spot it a mile off when they pulled up in their van.

Sammy looked at the paperwork, leaning it on the steering wheel. 'How come these fuckers think it's okay to stop paying their rent?' he said, peering through the windscreen at the house, which was looking dilapidated.

Bernie shrugged. 'Keeps us in a job booting them out.' He took his flask out and shook it at Sammy, offering him some.

'No, I do not want a drink out of that urinal you call a flask,' Sammy said.

'It was only that once, and I rinsed it out afterwards. See? I'll take the first drink.'

'I don't give a toss what you take. It's *your* flask, so you can drink your own pish.'

'My ma made it for me this morning,' Bernie said, looking offended.

'Let her drink it then.'

Bernie shook his head. 'I don't know.'

He drank some of the coffee and turned away to look out of the window and stuck his tongue out and dry heaved. An old woman who was walking by made a face back, and he could hear her say, 'Little bastard.'

Bernie thought his mother could do with some retraining when it came to rinsing out his flask. Or maybe he'd burn it.

'You know this piece of dirt hasn't paid rent in over eight months?' Sammy said.

'Stop complaining. When they get in arrears, they send us round to boot them out.' Bernie looked at his friend. 'What would you be doing if we weren't doing this?'

Sammy looked out the windscreen, thinking about it for a moment. 'Bus driver. What about you?'

'Porn star.'

'Jesus. Look at you: eighteen stone, forty if you're a day, and I bet you can't even see your dingdong, never mind swing it about in a filthy movie.'

'Forty? Come on now, Sammy, are you suffering from heatstroke or something? I'm twenty-nine. Forty? Good God.'

'You eat sausage rolls for breakfast, then you have a snack before we go into every house.' Sammy looked Bernie in the eye. 'When's the last time you were with a woman?'

'That's a bit personal.'

'We sit in a van together all day every day. We tell each other everything. I invited you to my niece's birthday party, and even carried you out to the taxi after you got blootered.'

'I got confused,' Bernie said. 'I forgot what niece it was who was having the party. I thought it was the eighteen-year-old, the one who's legally allowed to have some booze.'

'And when you arrived and the room was full of twelve-year-olds? That didn't ring alarm bells that you were at a wee lassie's party? That they were drinking juice and not voddy?'

'I was just being sociable with your dad.'

'We found him unconscious in the bathroom. After we found you having a piss on my mum's rose bushes.'

'Sammy, I've apologised to your mum many times since.'

'I've never been so affronted, let me tell you. Especially since the bairns were ready to start leaving. My niece is scarred for life now. When she asked why you were standing funny looking at the roses, I told her you were looking for an escaped hamster. Anybody else would have been locked up that day.'

'I thought I was in the toilet,' Bernie said in his defence.

'Christ, you were outside in the front garden. The old woman next door had a heart attack that day. Her son came round and found her on the living room floor. Luckily, she survived, and I'm not laying the blame at your door, but she could have been looking out of her window and saw a beast swinging it about.'

'Aw, come on there, Sammy, don't be saying things like that,' Bernie said.

'My mum says her neighbour won't set foot in a butcher's to this day. Every time she sees an advert for a sausage, she calls her in a panic.'

'Och away, you're just blowing smoke through your arse now.' Bernie screwed the lid back on his flask, trying not to smell the contents again. 'Let's get in that house and see what the score is.' He looked at Sammy again. 'Oh, and I'm seventeen stone.'

Sammy opened the driver's door and stepped out. 'When you stand on the talking scales, they say, "One at a time, please."'

'When you step on the scales, they say, "Get off me, ya fat bastard."'

'That's what your girlfriend says.'

'You think you're funny,' Bernie said.

Sammy locked the van, and they stood looking at the terraced house they were supposed to let themselves into. It looked dirty and abandoned, with no sign of any curtains or blinds. The windows looked like they were caked with dirt, and that was just on the inside.

'You never answered my question,' Sammy said. Then he turned to look at his friend.

'I'm going out this weekend with a woman, not that it's any of your business.'

'We tell each other everything. How wouldn't that be my business? What's her name?'

'Donna.'

'Not...Donna?'

Bernie smiled. 'Aye. *That* Donna.'

Sammy laughed. 'Good for you, mate.' Donna, one of the secretaries, was well-versed in entertaining men.

They walked up the path to the front door, and

Bernie took the set of keys out of his pocket, ready to unlock the door. Sammy held the papers and knocked, as per protocol. No answer. Then he had a look through the filthy living room window.

'It's empty. Except for a pile of shite.' He looked at his friend. 'Get it open, Bernie. Looks like he's done a moonlight.'

Bernie obliged and had the door open in a flash. They stepped in, still very much alert. In their experience, just because a house looked abandoned, that didn't mean it was. They both carried leather pouches that were kept closed by a drawstring, like taxi drivers carried, filled with pound coins. Not illegal to carry, but they had, on one occasion, given a druggie something to think about when he was sitting in the dentist's office after being on the receiving end of Sammy's pouch.

'You dropped one?' Sammy asked Bernie. 'Christ, did you have a Ruby Murray for breakfast again?'

'I only had a couple of mince pies.' Bernie looked at Sammy. 'I mean, a bowl of cornflakes.'

'Jesus, mate, I hate to say it, but maybe you should see a doctor about this. It's fucking rank.'

'Maybe he's just a minger. I mean, anybody who

uses old newspapers for a carpet isn't playing with a full deck.'

'Hoarders, Bernie, my son. Hoarders. It's an illness with them. I've watched hoarders shows on TV and they always say it's an illness.'

'It would have to be, wouldn't it? I mean, nobody in their right mind would want to live in a shithole like that.'

Sammy stood outside the closed living room door while Bernie walked along to the kitchen. He gently opened the door was looking through the tall gap between the door and the doorjamb. He put up a hand and Bernie stopped.

'I think there's somebody in there,' Sammy said.

'Well, get in there and see if it's our tenant.' Bernie said.

Sammy opened the door wider and went in. There was an armchair facing away from the window and somebody was sitting in it. Something that may or may not have been the tenant.

A long time ago.

TEN

Warriston Cemetery, Edinburgh

The motley crew were standing around talking to uniforms, some of them leaning on shovels and rakes, others holding shears and other gardening equipment.

'Remember this place from a few years ago?' Harry said as the car bumped over the rough track.

'How could I forget?' Miller said.

Hogweed stood tall by the side of the road, in among a field of tall grass, bushes and overgrown trees.

'Is it just me, or does it look like a film set where

that bunch of people is about to get wired into those uniforms?'

'Just you,' Miller said. 'That series they were filming in here is enough to occupy my brain without having other images in there.'

'How's Carol?' Harry asked as he pulled in behind the mortuary van. It was a question he'd asked over and over in the last six months since Miller's wife had come back into his life.

'Good.'

'I wasn't sure if you'd want to live round the corner from the flat where you and Carol lived. The one *you* rented out to me and then sold to me.'

'It brought back some good memories. I put the flat on the North Bridge up for sale and I have a few offers already.'

'How does your dad feel about that?' Harry asked. Miller's father – Jack, a retired DCI – lived just along the corridor with his crime writer girlfriend, Samantha Willis.

'He's fine. He wants me to be happy.'

'Big changes in your life, Frank. It's a lot to take in.' Harry looked out of the windscreen at the sky in the distance, where black clouds were lining up. 'Have you heard from Kim?'

Another question he kept on asking.

Miller shook his head. 'She's long gone now. I mean, she could have somehow called her dad and asked if everything was okay and if it was safe to come back to Edinburgh with the girls, but he's heard nothing. Kim wanted nothing more than to keep the girls protected, and I could have joined her, but now I'm glad I didn't. I'll let you in on a secret.'

Harry looked away from the clouds and at Miller. The car was still running, keeping the cold air flowing. 'What's that?'

'I never stopped loving Carol. We had a connection with each other that I just couldn't replicate with Kim. Although I loved Kim, of course, but it was different. Do you know what I mean?'

Harry nodded. 'I do.'

'Sometimes I can't believe Carol's back.'

'How do you feel about her working for Neil McGovern with Alex?'

'She loves it, and I'll always be nervous, but it was her choice. I'm not going to stand in her way.'

'Good man.'

Harry opened the driver's door and stepped out into the warmth of the afternoon. A gentle breeze was moving the trees and long grass. Miller got out the other side just as Calvin Stewart pulled up with Skellett in the passenger seat.

'When are you going to start fucking driving again?' Stewart said as they got out.

'I can hardly push a clutch pedal down when my knee's knackered now, can I?'

'I hope it's not so you can have a few swallies at lunchtime.'

'Like you and I used to have when we worked undercover in Glasgow, you mean?'

'Havering bastard. I never used to go drinking.' Stewart threw Skellett a look when Harry and Miller weren't looking.

They all walked over to the archway that led into the extension just as Finbar O'Toole walked out. He was dressed in his white suit with the hood up.

'Gentlemen,' he said. 'Where's the nice DS O'Shea?'

'She and Elvis are behind us,' Skellett said, 'but thanks to Stirling Moss, we made it here a bit quicker.'

'Faster *and* in one piece,' Stewart said. He looked around, then back at Skellett. 'You let one go?'

'Bog off.'

'It's fucking stinking in here.'

'I think you'll find the smell is being wafted from in there,' Finbar said.

'Lead on then, chief. Don't keep us in suspense,'

Stewart said, and they followed Finbar just as Lillian and Elvis pulled in behind the line of cars.

'You still wearing a brace then, Charlie?' Finbar asked.

'I am that, aye. Fucking thing is giving me gyp.'

Stewart held up a hand. 'We've heard enough of your pish. Fin, be a good lad and don't ask him about that rancid thing he straps to his leg, and I mean the brace.'

Finbar grinned. 'I had to wear one on my wrist, and they're no fun.'

'Oh aye. What were you doing to fuck up your wrist? Never mind. Scratch that. I don't think my mind could cope with two images of people wearing braces.'

Police tape had been rolled out, tied around a small tree and strung around some gravestones. Against the ivy bushes lay a blue anorak, light in colour and filthy. The victim wore dark trousers, but there was no evidence of shoes or socks. One arm lay outstretched, while the corpse lay on the other one.

'One of the old duffers threw his ring over there,' Finbar said as Lillian and Elvis came in.

'We started the party without you,' Stewart said to the two detectives.

'We're just about to get started, so don't worry,' Finbar said.

'Thank you, sir,' Lillian said. Elvis nodded to the small pathologist.

'There was no ID on him, so we don't know who he is just now.'

'Any way of telling how long he's been here?' Harry asked.

Finbar looked at him. 'He didn't die yesterday or the day before, obviously. It's hard for me to pin a number down, but we can do magic when we get to the mortuary.'

'I want to speak to the one who found him,' Stewart said. 'You and me, Harry. Charlie? Get interviewing the rest of the bunch.'

'Sir.'

The others trooped out, leaving Stewart and Harry alone with Finbar.

'Do you think he's been here all this time?' Harry asked.

'Probably. ' Finbar replied.

'Right, let's find the guy who found him,' Stewart said.

He and Harry went back through the archway, and Harry asked a uniform who found the body.

'That's him there, sir,' the uniform replied, pointing to Norman.

They went over to him. He looked to be in his forties and was wearing a sweater despite the warmth of the day.

'He gets a cold easily,' said the woman who was with him, as if reading their minds.

'And you would be?' Stewart said.

'Layla Hogg. This is my son, Norman. Is he in any trouble?'

Arnold made a scoffing noise, and the detectives turned to look at him.

'You think this is funny?' Harry asked him.

Arnold stopped smiling. 'Sorry. I just had a vision of Norman there being banged up with a group of hardened criminals.'

'Oh, shut up, Arnie. Poor Norman's shaking in his boots,' Layla said.

'We'd like to ask you some questions,' Stewart said to Norman. He eyed the man up: forties, living at home with Mummy. He'd be sure to ask for an alibi if they could nail down a date for when they thought the victim had died.

Norman shrugged. 'Okay.'

'You were through there on your own, or was somebody with you when you found the body?'

Stewart asked.

'I went on my own. To see how much work had to be done there.'

'Did you see the victim right away?' Harry asked.

Norman nodded. 'I saw the blue jacket. I came back out here to tell the others.'

'Did you cut back the grass and bushes around the body?'

Stewart looked at Arnold, who nodded. 'He did. He came out here and told us. He'd only been in there a few minutes before coming back out.'

'I can verify that,' Layla said. 'I know he's my son, but the others saw him too.'

'Did you cut the grass and ivy away from the body?' Harry asked.

Norman shook his head. 'It was already cut away. It was easy to spot the man.'

Stewart nodded. Although Norman could have been a killer, he didn't think the younger man had the intelligence to kill somebody and dump him here. But he never took anything for granted.

Finbar came out to join them. 'My assistants are going to transport him to the Cowgate, where Kate Murphy and I will do the postmortem.'

'Okay, Doc,' Stewart said and turned to Harry.

'Let's have a chat with some of the others, but at this point, I think it's just routine.'

'Agreed,' Harry said. 'But it's obvious the killer knew this place. Enough to know to hide the body in there. And for some reason, somebody came down here and cut the grass around the corpse, making sure it was exposed. Like they knew this group would be coming down here and somebody would find it.'

'Let's get their names through our system,' Stewart said. 'Starting with that guy Arnold.'

ELEVEN

Halifax, Yorkshire

DCI Tom Bailey stood in his living room, his battered tartan suitcase at his feet. DS Michael 'Biggie' Smalls sat on the couch, drinking a cup of coffee.

'Don't think we'll be stopping for a piss halfway,' Bailey said, nodding to the steaming mug.

'I've got a bladder like an iron boiler,' Biggie replied.

'Well, I've not.'

Biggie looked at Bailey. 'So what you're saying is, we *will* be stopping halfway, but it will be for you to have a piss.'

'Nobody likes a smartarse, lad.'

Cilla Bailey, Tom's wife, came thumping down the stairs.

'You would think she wears hobnailed boots,' Bailey said.

'What was that, love?' Cilla said, coming into the living room.

'I was just saying, I hope Biggie brought the polish for his boots.'

Cilla looked down at Biggie's feet. 'He's wearing shoes.'

'Shoes, boots, it's all the same.'

'Sorry, boss, we'll have to find some up there,' Biggie said.

'Aye, well, make sure he behaves himself, Michael,' Cilla said, adjusting the collar on her husband's jacket.

'Will do.' Biggie finished his coffee and took the mug through to the kitchen to rinse it out.

'I wish you would do that. Take your mug through.'

'I do when I remember, love,' Bailey said.

'Maybe you could work on doing some laundry sometime,' Cilla said, smiling at him.

'He'd have to incinerate his Ys,' Biggie said, coming back into the living room.

Cilla laughed.

'Don't encourage him,' Bailey said. 'Why don't you ask him to introduce you to his girlfriend? She's in his case with a bicycle pump.'

Cilla gently slapped his arm. 'I'm sure Michael does alright with the ladies. Don't you, son?'

'Goes without saying, Mrs B. In fact, if I was a bit older and that old codger you're married to had kicked off to sunnier climes...' Biggie grinned, leaving the sentence unfinished.

Cilla laughed.

'Don't mind him, blethering bastard,' Bailey said, making a face and shaking his head.

'Right, you better be off,' Cilla said.

'Why? Is the postman waiting round the corner?'

'Milkman, sweetheart. The postie was round last week.'

'I wondered why we had so much milk. And tell the postie to take that junk mail home wi' him. Just like he does with those bloody parcels.' Bailey picked up his suitcase and kissed his wife.

'You've got your underwear packed?' Cilla asked as Biggie stood up. 'The clean Y-fronts?'

'No, I grabbed some manky ones out of the laundry basket.'

'It wouldn't surprise me, love.' She turned to

Biggie. 'We've been married that long, there are no surprises.'

'Good to hear.' Except if your husband came home with VD. That might be the icing on the cake of all surprises.

'Right, you two, get off with you. I don't want you booting it up that A1. And I want a photo of that commendation you're getting. You too, Michael.'

'I'll be front and centre, Mrs B.'

'You heard my wife, Biggie; no driving that pocket rocket like you've got a firework up your arse. I want to get there in one piece, without my mother whispering for me to follow the light.'

Biggie grinned. 'Pocket rocket. It's a Nissan I have now. I got rid of that little Ford.'

'You didn't want to look like a little twat boy racer anymore?'

'Nah. Just time I got something sensible.' Biggie didn't want to tell his boss that he had lost control of it and shoved it through a fence, nearly shitting himself in the process.

'Well, take care. That was very nice of the pathologist to let you use her house while you're there,' Cilla said.

'Aye, well, she spends most of her time at Jimmy

Craig's, so we'll have the place to ourselves,' Bailey said.

'She must be happy that you took care of the bastard who was stalking her.'

'Aye, she is that. Nice woman. You'd like her. Maybe we'll go up there for a break one day and I'll introduce her.'

'I'd like that.' She kissed him again and turned to Biggie. 'Look after this old bastard. I don't know what I'd do without him.'

'Jesus, woman, don't get all soft on me now,' Bailey said.

'Will do, Mrs B. He's in good hands.'

They left Bailey's house and got into the Qashqai.

'Nice little motor,' Bailey said. 'You shite yourself when you went through that fence with that little mental thing you used to drive?'

'How di–?'

'A friend in traffic. We had a bloody good laugh about it. After I knew you were okay, like. Plus, the lass from CID you've been seeing told her pals.'

'Oh God. She said she wouldn't say anything.'

'That's what you get for being a southern git who couldn't drive a pig with a stick.'

Biggie had no reply. Although his girlfriend was now in danger of not getting the tartan doll he'd thought he would buy for her.

Bailey had the front seat reclined before Biggie had a chance to put the car in gear. He was snoring by the time they reached the end of the street.

TWELVE

'Oh, this is exciting,' Isla said from the back seat. 'Two trips in the car in one day. Not even my dad managed that.'

Craig pulled in behind the police van parked on Linnwood Drive, a little street off the main road. He hadn't been to this part of Leven in a long time. It was on the north side of the town, a quiet part that could do with some TLC.

Dan Stevenson was in the front passenger seat, and he let go of his seatbelt as Craig turned off the engine.

'I knew a lassie who lived in Leven,' he said. 'Long time ago.'

'Round this part?' Isla said, smiling and leaning forward.

'No. Down a bit. Waggon Road.'

'What was she like?'

'She was nice, but we just didn't have anything in common.'

'Why did you go out with her, then?' Craig asked, his hand on the door handle, ready to open it.

'We met in a pub and she liked to…you know…'

'What?' Isla said. 'Go ten-pin bowling? Running? Rock climbing? What?'

'Aye, what did she like to do?' Craig asked.

'You know what? I'm not telling you two anything again,' Dan said, getting out of the car.

Craig turned round to Isla and laughed. 'You're a bad lassie, you know that?'

'Of course I do.'

They got out and walked round to the main road, where a uniform was standing at the end of the path that led up to the front door. She nodded to the detectives.

Craig saw Annie Keller's Audi parked further along the road and saw her moving about through the living room window.

Inside, she was talking to the head of forensics, Stan Mackay. They turned to look at Craig and the others when they entered the room.

'Smell that?' Annie said from behind her mask.

'I do, indeed,' Craig replied, and he and the other two detectives each pulled out a disposable mask and put it on.

Annie and Mackay stepped aside, and then Craig saw the form sitting in the chair. The room was filled with rubbish, like squatters had camped here and trashed the place, but then Craig realised this was more of a hoarder situation. Dust covered every surface, and newspapers and other rubbish covered the floor so that no floor covering could be made out.

Craig took a step forward and looked more closely at the corpse sitting in the armchair. This was the only piece of furniture in the room. There was no TV, settee, side table or anything else that might have made up a normal living room. There was nothing else on the chair, no sign that any piece of rubbish had ever resided on it. Just the man with decomposing features.

'Natural causes?' Craig asked. If it were, they could all go back to the station and write a quick report and have it filed by knocking-off time.

'Hell no,' Annie said.

Mackay shook his head. 'I've seen some stuff,

Jimmy, but this is brutal.' He too was talking from behind a mask.

Craig could see that the corpse's trousers were open, like he had sat down to watch TV and had felt they were too tight.

'Somebody cut his genitalia off,' Annie said. 'The whole lot. In the absence of any other obvious marks, I'd say he bled out. But of course, upon further examination, he might prove me to be a liar.'

'Are you going to do the postmortem today?' Isla asked.

Annie looked at her. 'I know I'm good, young lady, but I'm not that good.' She shook her head. 'No, we're full to capacity. Both Dunfermline and Kirkcaldy mortuaries. Dundee are a no-go too. Edinburgh said they'll take him. I spoke to Finbar and he said they would take him today, no problem. He said he and Kate can fit him in tomorrow first thing.'

'Jesus, is it the hot weather that's filling up your fridges?' Dan asked.

'Sudden deaths, two car accidents with four victims, a child drowning, an electrocution with somebody trying to save money by doing some DIY. I've never had so much fun.'

'How long do you think he's been sitting there?' Craig asked.

'Not long. You can see from the fabric of the chair, all his bodily fluids spilled out somewhere else, and only some have soaked into the chair. Somebody placed him there.'

'Who found him?'

'Two guys from the council who were here to evict the tenant,' Mackay said.

'And this is the tenant?' Isla said.

Mackay nodded. 'At least the name on the eviction notice is the same as the one in the wallet we took from this man. Eddie Hay.'

Craig nodded. 'I want to go and talk to them.'

He walked out of the living room and left the house. The sky was clear and the air warm, but there was a persistent wind finding its way in from the sea.

Bernie and Sammy were talking to a uniform, and Craig was directed to them by another officer.

'You two found the body?' he asked.

Bernie nodded. 'He was just sitting there when we went in.'

'He'd hardly be dancing,' Sammy said, tutting, showing why he was the one earning the big bucks. 'Yes, we went in to evict the tenant and that...*thing*... was sitting there waiting for us.'

'How long had the eviction been in effect?'

'It starts months before. If all communication

fails and no money is forthcoming, then we get sent round to evict the tenant.'

'Including knocking the door off its hinges, if need be,' Bernie added, nodding. 'Oh aye, there's no fuc...I mean, messing about at this stage. The council wants its house back and that's what we're here to do, take it back. Him in there, he was just another sponger who thought the taxpayer should fund his way of living.'

'Okay, Bernie, we don't need another rant,' Sammy said.

'What's the name?' Craig asked.

'Eddie Hay. I don't know his background like you might, but he was hardly an upstanding member of the community. It's getting worse, unfortunately.'

'Have either of you been here before?' Craig asked.

'Not me,' Sammy said, quickly wanting to distance himself from this scene.

Bernie shook his head. 'Me neither.'

'Right, I'll need you both to come along to Glenrothes and make a statement.'

Both men nodded. Craig turned back to the house and walked forward to meet Annie, who had come out of the house, still in her white suit.

'Drinks tonight with Tom and Biggie, then back to your place so we can celebrate in style.' She grinned at him.

'Sounds good to me.' He smiled back at her. 'That was good of you to let them stay in your house.'

'I wouldn't let just anybody stay there. I mean, if they were members of a biker gang, I might have politely said no. But since they helped catch that bastard who was stalking me, it was the least I could do.'

'I'm looking forward to having a drink with them.'

'Tom said they'd be here about four thirty.' She looked at her watch. 'Time to give Mr Hay a ride in a mortuary van to our overflow fridges, then he'll be taken across to Edinburgh tomorrow for his appearance at the Cowgate.'

They were silent for a moment before Craig spoke. 'That was personal. What they did to him.'

'Oh, I know. I've been doing this long enough to know the difference. There's remnants of a material round his wrists, like they tied him up and probably took their time with him.'

Isla and Dan came out of the house and approached them.

'You two are like teenagers,' Isla said, grinning. 'What do you think, Dan?'

'Leave me out of this. DCI Craig has to write my annual appraisal before sending it upstairs. You can go out on a limb if you want, but I'm saying nothing.'

'Go on, Dan, we'll keep it right here,' Annie said. 'Any observations?'

'Nope. I have nothing to say.'

Annie grinned and looked at the entrance to the garden. 'I bet *he* will, though.'

DSup Mark Baker shambled in, looking like a half-shut knife.

'Thanks for joining us, Mark,' Annie said. 'I'm glad to see you kept it casual dress. Or at least, kept the scruffy bastard look. We were all thinking of chipping in for an iron for your birthday.'

'Thanks, Annie. My birthday was two months ago.'

'Next year.' She grinned at him. 'How's the love life going?'

'Time and a place. This is not it.'

'You're still coming along to my party on Saturday, aren't you?' she asked.

'If I can find a shirt that's not creased.'

'That's what Marks and Spencer is for. Buy a new one.'

'Oh boy, I should have looked for a shirt in the charity shop when I was in there buying your birthday present.'

She chuckled. 'Good one. I hope it's something like a backscratcher. That would be easier to insert into you.'

Baker looked at Craig, who shrugged. 'Don't look at me, boss. I wouldn't want to bandy words with her.'

'I suppose we should call a truce,' Baker said, looking back at Annie.

'I think that would be a good idea on your part, chief. It would only have resulted in you having a body part sewed back on.'

'You better sleep with one eye open,' Baker said to Craig. 'But anyway, I'd like a word.'

Craig nodded and then Baker walked away.

'See? One eye open, he said,' Craig said to Annie. 'He obviously knows you a lot better than I do.'

'You make it sound like a challenge,' she said, grinning.

'Just remember, I don't have a sewing kit.'

Craig walked over to where Baker was standing. 'What's up, boss?'

'That victim in there?' Baker pointed over his shoulder with a thumb.

'What about him?'

'He's a rapist. Eddie Hay was arrested for raping a woman, but he said it was consensual after they'd been to a nightclub in Kirkcaldy. It was a case of "she said, he said". CCTV showed them leaving together, and other men came forward to say she had been flirting with them until she went home with Hay. She couldn't remember anything that happened when she woke up feeling like crap.'

'Date rape?'

'We'll never know. He walked free from court. Not proven.'

'You think this was a revenge killing?'

'Could be,' Baker said.

'Then we should be talking to the girl's family. Hay's family too.'

'Hay didn't have any family. Neither did his victim. Last I heard, she was working as a nurse.'

'What was Hay's occupation?'

'He was a bus driver.'

'He could have come into contact with his victims if they were on his bus, then he sought them out at a club.'

'To play devil's advocate, he might have been innocent,' Baker said.

'Somebody didn't think so. Let's go and talk to the victim. Do you remember her name?'

'Suzie Carr. I'll look up her details, see if she can provide us with an alibi.'

'Right. Let me know. I'd like to be in on the interview,' Craig said.

'You'll be doing the interview. Take Dan with you. He was on the original case. I have some shite to do in my office. I just wanted to come along and have a look at the scene.'

'Fair enough.'

'What time is Tom Bailey due?' Baker asked.

'Four-ish.'

'Having a wee swallie tonight?'

'Having a few drinks in the golf club, then Annie and I are having a night in together since it's her birthday. You want to come along for a drink?'

'I wish I could.'

'What's stopping you, boss?' Craig asked.

Baker looked around to make sure nobody was listening. 'The lassie I'm seeing? Well, she –'

'The psycho?' Craig said, interrupting.

'Aye, aye, the psycho. Well, she's not only off her

heid, she's jealous as well. She's already accused me of seeing other women.'

'Wait; you met her on an app, and you started seeing her. Did you tell her it was an exclusive thing you had going on?'

'Not in so many words. She seems to think so, but it's a site where you just meet women, everybody has a good time, and you move on. That's the general rule with this site. Everybody knows that. But she seems to think she's my girlfriend now.'

'Maybe you should tell her that it's not as exclusive as she thought.'

'I've dug myself a hole here, son. I mean, on the one hand, it's nice to have a woman fawn over me, but then there are a lot of restrictions. She wants us to have a drink tonight. I would have come along to meet the lads from Yorkshire, but if Jane found out, she'd go mental.'

'Good God. I wouldn't like to be in your shoes.'

'Thanks. That doesn't give me a bad feeling in the pit of my stomach.' Baker took in a breath and blew it out. 'The sex is good, though.'

'I'll have the mason chip that into your headstone after she murders you in your sleep. And let me point you towards the man in there; he's had his whole kit chopped off.'

'What? Even his...?'

'Everything. Gone. That'll be you next if you're not careful.'

'Jesus.'

'Maybe you should get an alibi for Jane after you find out the time of death, which wasn't recent. That man in there is literally about to explode.'

'Mother of Christ,' Baker said. 'You don't suppose he was one of her boyfriends? I mean, Hay was the right age for her. I'm going to delve into his background. And hers.'

'I thought it was against policy to look up somebody for personal use?'

'It is. But I think I remember seeing her name in connection with the Hay case, so I'm within my rights to look her up.'

'Oh, okay,' Craig said, playing along.

Baker shuffled away into the house to have a look at the victim.

'He's crapping himself over that lassie, isn't he?' Dan said, coming up to Craig.

'He told you about her too?'

'Aye. In the pub. He likes going out with her, but he said her mood swings are mental.'

'No doubt she'll be coming along to Saturday night's do at the golf club. I hope to Christ she behaves herself,' Craig said. 'He also said he wants us to interview Hay's victim, Suzie Carr.'

'I remember the case well. She was convinced that he drugged her and raped her.'

'Get her details, Dan, and we'll see if we can talk to her.'

'Will do.'

Craig spoke to Annie one more time before leaving the scene with Dan.

THIRTEEN

In the end, Tom Bailey and Biggie stopped for a pee twice. And then for a haggis supper when they decided to divert to South Queensferry.

'You've got to admit, the Scottish know how to make a good supper,' Bailey said as they leaned against the railings on the promenade, looking towards the Forth Rail Bridge.

'They do that. I'd be a fat bastard like you if I lived up here. I'd have this for dinner every night.'

'This is all muscle, son,' Bailey said, holding the supper in one hand while taking a bottle of Irn-Bru out of his pocket to wash it down. He'd already taken the cap off, but it hung in there, not wanting to let go. 'How are things going with your girlfriend?'

'Everything's fine. What makes you ask?'

'I'm a Nosy bastard. And because Cilla's been asking and she'll nip my head until I ask you.' Bailey looked at Biggie, who he regarded as part of his family. His own little boy had died years ago, and now Cilla felt like Biggie was her own.

'Ah. Well, in that case, there's no point in lying anymore. We decided to go our own ways.'

'She kicked you into touch.' Bailey rolled up the paper and walked over to a bin and dumped it. 'That was fooking good.'

'I wouldn't exactly say, kicked into touch,' Biggie said. 'She told me that she didn't want things to get serious between us, and that we should cool things for a while.'

'How do you feel about that?'

Biggie finished his haggis supper and dumped the rubbish into the bin. He came back and stood looking out to sea. 'There's plenty more fish in there, big man.'

'Somebody for everybody, even an ugly little bastard like you.' Bailey grinned at him.

'Something like that. Hey, we've been invited to Annie's party on Saturday, so maybe there will be some nice Scottish lassies there looking for a good time.'

'Did she say there would be somebody there

with a guide dog?' Bailey laughed. 'Come on, Romeo, let's get over to Dunfermline and find this street where Annie's house is.'

DI Max Hold was working a cold case with DS Gary Menzies and DC Jessie Bell in the station in Glenrothes.

'I heard it was a bad one down the road,' Hold said to Craig.

'I don't think I'll be wanting any dinner, put it that way. He's been dead a long time, and somebody had it away with a pair of shears or something and cut his pieces off.'

'Jesus. That made me shrink a little bit.'

'You and me both, son. How's your case coming along?'

'Slow and steady.'

Craig looked at his watch. 'The Yorkshire boys should be here in a wee while. I just want to check something, then I'll be leaving for the day.'

'I'll bash on with this case.'

'Righto.' Craig waved Isla over and handed her a folder. 'This is a copy of the Stephen Colby report. It's from after he walked out of court a free man.

When they arrested him and charged him as a serial killer.'

'Okay. You want me to read it now?'

'Yes. I'm going to read through it too and we can compare notes. I'll be in my office.'

'Okay, boss. Give me a shout when you're finished and we can compare notes.'

Craig went into his office and took out his own copy of the report. He could have read it on the computer, but everything was done on the computer these days. Sometimes it was nice to have the papers in his hands.

He sat back in his chair and put his feet up on the desk and began reading about Stephen Colby.

FOURTEEN

Thirty years ago

DCI Kenny Campbell would have pulled his hair out if he'd had any left. Instead, he settled for running a hand over his bald head.

'There has to be something,' he said. 'I've just been up to see the chief constable, and he's just about having a canary. Of course, I got chewed out like it was my fucking fault. Now, here I am, chewing you lot out.'

There was murmuring between the other detectives, side glances and tutting.

Campbell waved a hand at them. 'Calm down. It's Captain Pugwash who's moaning. But so far, there are five women missing, and nobody has heard anything from them.' He pointed to the whiteboard, where photos and names were looking back at them.

'As of this moment, their husbands haven't heard a thing from them,' DI Lou Cairns said. His stomach grumbled. Dinnertime had come and gone, and somebody had suggested they go for a fish supper and that had made it worse. It was going on seven now, darkness had kicked in hours ago and it made it seem like they'd been working for a week. But getting the women back was more important.

Suddenly, the incident room door burst open.

'We've got another one. She managed to get away, and she got the bastard's licence plate. It's fucking Colby's,' DS Angie White said.

They all jumped up from their desks, those who were still sitting, Campbell and Cairns joining them.

It was freezing out, but Campbell was sweating like a bastard as he ran to his car, Cairns right beside him. The others jumped into their cars and they took off. Campbell had bumped into their DSup in the corridor, an old codger with a broken leg, but he was just as enthusiastic as the rest of them. He told Campbell the search warrant had been issued and was hot off the press. A uniformed patrol would meet them there, along with a bunch of others, ready to tear Colby's house apart.

When they got to the street in Dunfermline, it was shock and awe. Colby's car was on the street outside his parents' house, where he lived. The house was a semi on the outskirts of the town, in a quiet street.

'You know the routine, son,' Campbell said to one of the uniforms. 'One knock on the door, then after two, take the fucking thing off its hinges.'

Colby's father answered the door after knock two, and Campbell tried to hide the disappointment he felt on not being able to see the door fly off its hinges into their hallway.

'What do you lot fucking want now?' the man said.

'Brian Colby?' Campbell said.

'You know fine well it is, ignorant bastard,' Stephen Colby's father said.

'I have a warrant to search your house and all outbuildings on the property.' Campbell slapped a sheet of paper into the man's chest.

'What if I don't want you to?'

'Tough shit,' Cairns said. 'And if you fucking try and stop us, we'll steamroller right over the top of you.'

'What is it, Brian?' Stephen's mother said, coming to the door.

'You know what this shower of bastards are like,' Brian said, turning to his wife.

Campbell had had enough chitchat and he barged in, Cairns right behind him, followed by a dozen uniforms.

'Just you mind my china,' the wife said.

'Where's your son?' Campbell asked her.

'Upstairs.'

Campbell nodded to Cairns, who stormed up the stairs with uniforms at his back. Campbell went into the living room as more uniforms started rummaging around in drawers in the china cabinet.

'You think my son's hiding some women in a drawer,' Brian said, scoffing. 'I told you the last time you were round here, he hasn't touched any women.'

'You would know where he is every minute, then?' Campbell said, getting in the other man's face. 'Like where he was tonight?'

Brian looked confused for a minute. 'He wasn't out tonight.'

'Why don't you ask him?' Cairns said, manhandling Stephen Colby into the room.

'Were you out tonight?' his mother asked. 'I didn't see you go out.'

'I just popped out for a pack of ciggies, Mum. I wasn't even gone five minutes.'

'We'd like you to come to the station to answer some questions,' Campbell said, hoping the bastard would refuse and put himself even more in the spotlight.

'Okay, that's fine. But if it's about that lassie, I just asked her for a light because I'd forgotten to buy a lighter.'

'Don't say any more,' Cairns warned. 'You haven't been cautioned.'

'She started shouting at me. I don't know if she heard me or not, but then she started shouting for her friends. Then screaming.' Colby's face was falling. 'I only asked for a light.'

'Don't say any more, son,' Brian said. 'I'll call a solicitor.'

The family sat around in the living room while the police officers turned their lives upside down. Campbell was in and out, moving from room to room, trying not to be a pain in the arse, but nobody would tell him to his face that he *was*.

It all kicked off when somebody got a chair and stood up on it to push open the attic hatch. Campbell went to have a look and saw a light being switched on in the attic. Then another Uniform was up, and

Campbell heard the young man yell out; obviously, he'd banged his shin. There were no ladders or other means to climb in through the square hole in the ceiling; it required brute strength.

'Banged my fucking leg,' he heard the man say and there was a snort of laughter.

'Clumsy bastard.'

'Keep it down; Campbell's downstairs,' he heard the second one say.

'Campbell's on the fucking landing,' Campbell said in a loud voice. 'Less of the hilarity and get a bloody move on.'

'That's you clowning about, arsehole,' the second one said, thinking that by lowering his voice, he wouldn't be heard.

'Ya wee fanny. I managed to get up without ripping my baws off.'

Cairns came up the stairs. 'How's it going?'

'If Laurel and Hardy up there would get a bloody move on, we would be finished in half the time.'

'Up here!' one of Uniforms shouted from the attic. 'Oh Christ!'

Then he appeared above, looking down at them. 'You need to see this, sir.'

'Give us a hand,' Campbell said, putting one foot

on the chair. He clearly wasn't as lithe as the two younger men, who had managed the climb on their own. Cairns held on to Campbell's arm, and then Campbell got a pull-up from one of the uniforms, who was much stronger.

Cairns got up under his own steam.

'What are we looking at?' Campbell asked.

'Over there, sir,' the Uniform said, pointing to a trunk.

Campbell ducked his head so as not to bump it on one of the rafters. The lid had been lifted by the second Uniform, but the inside of the trunk was facing away from Campbell. He walked forward and looked into the trunk from the side. There was a pile of women's clothes, including underwear, but it was what was lying on top of the clothes that his eyes fixed on.

A human ear.

He turned to Lou Cairns. 'Get down there, quick, and arrest that bastard.' Then, out loud to nobody in particular: 'Just out buying cigarettes, my arse.'

FIFTEEN

Now

Craig lifted his feet off his desk and placed the folder on it. Then he saw Isla get up from her desk and knock on his door.

'Come in,' he said, and she entered.

'What did you make of that, boss?' she asked.

'To be honest, he was put away on circumstantial evidence, which I'm surprised about. No DNA, no prints, no bodies, no confession.'

'The trunk with the body part and clothing is pretty damning, though.' She sat down opposite Craig. 'The woman was identified as Rae Holburn from one of the dresses, one of the missing women, but what about the others?'

'They were never found or heard from again. It was assumed he killed them all, but no proof was ever brought forward.' He looked at her. 'What if his father was the killer?' he asked her.

She shook her head. 'They cross-checked the dates with his movements, and he had alibis for the times the women went missing. He was in the pub or some social club. He was on the darts team, surrounded by his friends. It was enough for them to rule him out.'

'Did you see who the judge was who put Stephen Colby away?' he asked her.

'William Keller.'

Craig nodded. 'After what happened with Keller's son and Colby, McCallum was going to throw the book at him. Which he did. Life in the psychiatric hospital.'

'You think Colby was set up?'

'I'm not sure what I think just now, Isla. It just seems they were keen to put him away. Which leaves the question: if Colby is innocent, then who killed those women?'

'And who would want to frame Colby, if indeed that's what happened?' Isla said.

'And let's not forget he said that one of them was still alive. How would he know that?'

'Maybe he saw her in the hospital? A visitor, maybe?'

'Could be. I'd like you to do some research, Isla: find out how many, if any, men were charged with murder and the case was found not proven. Go back thirty years.'

'I'll get right on that, boss,' she said, standing up.

'See how many McCallum presided over.'

'Will do.'

As Isla left his office, Craig sat back in his chair. Six women had disappeared, none of them heard from again, presumed murdered and hidden somewhere.

Craig's phone rang. 'Hello?'

'I didn't catch you napping, did I?' Annie said.

'You did actually. I was just about to get the secret bottle out of my desk drawer and have at it.'

'That bad a day?'

'Just something that's puzzling, that's all. But listen, I have a request.'

'Well then, Jimmy Craig, how can a woman resist such persuasion?'

Craig laughed. 'I know it's your birthday and we're meeting Bailey for a few drinks, but do you think we could pop in and see your uncle before then, on the way home?'

'Of course. I'm not sure if he will know who we are, but we can pop in. Any special reason?'

'No. Well, yes. I just wanted to have a wee talk with him. See if I can stir up any memories.'

'That's fine. I'm about to leave work anyway. You want me to meet you over there?'

'Okay,' Craig said.

'I had a call from Tom. He and Biggie are in Dunfermline. I'll meet them at my house and give them the keys, and then meet you at the home.'

Annie gave him the address, and he hung up. He wasn't sure what he was looking for, but he thought it would be interesting to talk to William Keller.

He spoke to Max Hold before he left and asked him to do some research.

SIXTEEN

Annie lived in a new development, where the gardens were smaller than those of houses built years ago, but she liked it. So did Tom Bailey.

'This is some place you've got here, lass,' he said. He called her *lass*, though he was only a couple of years older than her.

'Thank you,' she said, hugging him. Biggie stepped forward and hugged her too.

'Glad to see you both again, even though it's only been a few weeks.'

'We couldn't keep away,' Biggie said. 'Besides, Tom here needs his fill of haggis and Irn-Bru. Which he had in South Queensferry.'

'Damn fine stuff is haggis,' Bailey confirmed.

'I don't partake, to be honest,' Annie said. 'I've never liked it.'

'That's sacrilege, surely?' Bailey said, taking his tartan suitcase out of the boot. Biggie grabbed his own holdall.

'Only if you listen to certain people. Come in, I'll show you around. Then I have to leave to visit my uncle who's in a nursing home. He's got late-stage dementia, and he doesn't have long.'

'Jesus, I'm sorry to hear that, Annie,' Bailey said.

She unlocked the door and showed them into her house. It was clean and fresh. 'Living room on the right, kitchen through the back, dining room on the left, toilet down the hall, upstairs are the bedrooms and the bathroom. The main bedroom has an en-suite, so you won't have to share a shower. If you see what I mean. Not at the same time, obviously.'

'I know some mucky buggers are into that stuff, but the lad and I don't dabble in that.' Bailey looked at Biggie, who was checking out a print on the wall. Bailey elbowed him.

'Christ. What was that for?'

'I was just telling Annie that we...Oh, never mind.' Bailey looked back at Annie. 'Trust me, I'm married, and he's engaged to a lady who came through the post and is harder to blow up than a beach ball, so he says.'

'Don't talk crap.' Biggie looked at Annie. 'I'm seeing somebody, Annie, trust me, and if I was going down another road, he certainly wouldn't be on my radar.'

Bailey looked at him. 'Just stop talking now.'

'Bagsy the master bedroom,' Biggie said.

'It's technically known as the primary bedroom these days, ignorant little bastard. And you're bagsying fook all. Show me the way to the primary, Annie, if you please. I want to get unpacked.'

'Why don't you get her to show you where she keeps her blowtorch so you can launder your skids?'

'Belt up.'

Annie went upstairs ahead of them, and she showed Bailey the primary when he got up to the landing. 'That's my bedroom there, but I'll be over at Jimmy's, so make yourself at home,' she said.

'Thanks, Annie.' Bailey turned to Biggie. 'You better have remembered them strip things that go across your nose to help you breathe at night.' Bailey turned back to Annie. 'The last time we had to stay overnight, we were in a guest house, and I was dreaming I was in *The Texas Chainsaw Massacre*. It was that little southern git snoring his head off across the landing.'

Annie laughed. 'There's four bedrooms to choose from, so I'm sure you won't have to be next to each other. I mean, in the rooms next to each other.'

'I know what you meant, Annie, but you're starting to give me a complex.'

'It's those vibes you give off to women,' Biggie said. 'If you weren't married to Cilla, well...' He left the sentence unfinished.

'Shut your hole.'

Annie laughed. 'I'll let you boys sort yourselves out.' She handed Bailey the keys. 'Drinks at the golf club around seven thirty?' she said. 'I'll text you the address, but if you get a taxi, the driver will know where to go.'

'Thanks for that.'

Biggie went into another room across the hall. 'Drinks are on us,' he said. 'And when I say *us*, I mean him.'

Bailey made a face. 'It's going on our expenses. I'll work it in somehow. I know a lass in accounts.'

'Rumour has it that he keeps a ten-shilling note in his pocket,' Biggie said. 'Left over from the days when he used to put his hand in his pocket.'

Bailey shook his head. 'His Irn-Bru obviously

went to his head. All the fizziness makes him talk shite.'

Annie smiled and patted his arm. 'Make yourselves at home. The fridge is well stocked and there's beer in there.'

'Bagsy any lager,' Biggie said.

'Use that word one more time and you'll be getting a boot in the bagsy.'

'Yeah, yeah.'

SEVENTEEN

Annie was standing leaning against her car, a cigarette in her mouth, when Craig pulled in beside her. He'd never been to this nursing home before. He raised his eyebrows when he saw the cigarette.

'What?' she said, taking it out. 'It's not as if I was going to smoke it. It's not smoking unless it's lit.'

'It's the temptation. It's in your mouth, and I bet your hand is on your lighter in your pocket.'

She took her hand out of her pocket. 'See, that's where you're wrong, copper. And you can't prove otherwise.'

He grinned at her and walked across and kissed her.

'My-my. We are getting bolder, aren't we? But I'm not complaining. Do it again,' Annie said.

'Sorry, but I like to leave the ladies wanting a little bit more.'

'That doesn't say much for your reputation,' Annie said, grinning.

'Dammit. That backfired on me. Now, let's get inside before it goes down a road I don't want it to go down.'

She took his arm as they walked across the car park. They had clocked off being colleagues. Now they were friends. Then she noticed somebody sitting in a car further along.

'There's Jackson,' she said.

Craig looked around. 'Am I supposed to know who that is?'

'Of course not, but let me introduce you to him.' She walked over to the hatchback and rapped on the window. The man in the driver's seat spun his head round and almost screamed. Instead, he rolled the window down.

'Jesus, Annie, I think I shat myself. If you were hoping to see that, mission accomplished.'

Annie laughed. 'Jackson Clover, this is my friend DCI Jimmy Craig. Jimmy, this is Garfield's brother.'

Craig shook the hand the man offered. 'Although I don't know who Garfield is.'

Annie grinned. 'Oh yeah, I forgot, you haven't

met Garfield yet. He's the male attendant who helps to look after Uncle Bill.'

'Huge guy. Ginger-heided. Daft as a brush. You can't miss him. Bit of a radge at times. Just don't tell him I told you that,' Jackson said.

'Lips are sealed,' Annie said, mimicking drawing a zip along her lips and throwing the key away.

'Still having trouble with the smoking?' Jackson asked her.

'How did you know?'

'Standing outside your car with an unlit ciggie in your mouth told me the whole story.'

'See?' Craig said. 'Other people know what you're like.'

'Oh, away with you both. Just for that, I'm going to go home tonight and light one up,' Annie said.

Inside, the home smelled like Craig imagined all nursing homes smelled: disinfectant.

A big ginger-haired man smiled when he saw them coming. 'Annie! To what do we owe this surprise visit?'

'It's my birthday.'

'Well, many happy returns and all that.' The man gave her a hug. 'And who is this fine young man you have in tow?'

'This is DCI James Craig. My boyfriend,' Annie said without hesitation. 'Garfield Clover.'

'Pleased to meet you, DCI Craig.'

'Likewise.'

'Has this little scallywag told you all about me then?'

'No, she hasn't,' Craig said. He looked at the man, built like a brick shithouse with hands like shovels; he looked like he weighed twice what Craig weighed.

'I'll have to remedy that,' Garfield said. 'But hear this: if there's any such thing as Oscars for nursing home aides, then I shall, indeed, be expecting to see my name on a nomination.'

Annie laughed. 'I'm open to bribery.'

'Dear oh dear. In front of James here too. He'll have you in handcuffs in a heartbeat.'

'I hope so,' Annie said, grinning.

'What a wee besom. I've never heard such stuff in my life. I'm going to go and have a lie-down. But before you go and see your uncle, do you have a spare ciggie?'

'I gave you one yesterday and you said it was a keeper, but you went away to smoke it.'

'What can I say, Annie? I'm weak.'

'Sorry, Garfield. I'm not going to encourage your habit.' She smiled at him.

'Oh man. If my girlfriend knew I was smoking at work, she'd go off her nut.'

'Don't tell her,' Craig suggested.

'Now why didn't I think of that?' Garfield said.

'You're still coming to the party on Saturday?' Annie asked him.

'We wouldn't miss it for the world.'

'Great.'

'I look forward to introducing my other half to you, DCI James,' Garfield said.

'I look forward to it,' Craig replied.

They fist-bumped, and Garfield walked off in the opposite direction.

'Nice guy,' Craig said.

'He is. He takes care of my uncle. Salt of the earth.'

Bill Keller was sitting in a chair watching TV when they went into his room.

'Uncle Bill,' Annie said, smiling.

The man turned to look at her. 'Can I help you?'

'It's me, Annie.'

'Oh, Annie! I didn't see you there. Come away in.'

'Bill, I've brought somebody to see you; this is my friend, Jimmy.'

Bill scrunched his eyes at her. 'He looks a bit old to be your friend, Annie. You should really have friends your own age.'

'Oh, he's fine. We're almost the same age. I'm forty-five today,' Annie said.

'You are? I thought you were going to be twenty-five. Oh well, happy birthday. Sit down, sit down. Nice to meet you, Jimmy.'

Annie turned to Craig. 'He's a little bit more lucid today. They changed his meds a few days ago. Something to take the edge off.'

Craig nodded to her. 'Good to meet you too, sir,' he said to the old man.

'Sit down then, son; you're making the place look like a pigsty.'

Craig sat on the bed, while Annie pulled over a smaller chair.

'I'm going to keep the TV on,' Bill said. 'These walls have ears.'

'What are you watching?' Annie said.

They could both see the changes coming over the man's face.

'What do you mean, what am I watching? What's that got to do with the price of cheese?

Stupid woman.'

Annie looked at Craig, who just nodded slightly towards her, a nod that said, *This is to be expected* and *Ask him while he's talkative.*

'Listen, Bill, I was thinking about what you said the other day.'

'About the price of cheese?'

'No, about Albert Fish.'

Bill sucked in a breath and looked wildly around himself. 'Is he here? In the hospital? I knew I saw that bastard the other day. Did you see him?'

'No,' Annie said, keeping her voice steady. 'You said you saw him.'

'I did? Where?'

'In here. You said there's a killer walking about in here,' Annie said. Craig just looked at the old man.

'He is. I saw him. Looking right back at me.'

'Where is he now?'

Bill looked blankly at her for a moment, then a fire lit up behind his eyes. 'He was in here.' His voice was a whisper now. 'Stephen Colby's in prison, did you know that? He was sentenced last week. I made sure the bastard paid.'

'What did Colby do, Bill?' Annie asked.

Bill stared off into space for a few moments.

'Annie! When did you come in? And Monty's with you. Good to see you again, son.'

Monty was Annie's ex-husband.

'Good to see you too, Bill,' Craig said. 'You know who was asking for you the other day? Stephen Colby.'

Bill's face fell. 'Was he now. Little bastard. But can you keep a secret?'

'Of course I can.'

'When you're a judge, you can do things. Things that other people can't. *Punish* people.' He tapped the side of his nose. 'You know what I did?'

'Now then, what's going on here? Having a party without me?' A young female nurse stood in the doorway, smiling. 'I'm Michelle. I'm helping out tonight because we're short-staffed.'

'I'm Annie, his niece. This is my partner, Jimmy.'

'Nice to meet you both.'

Bill looked at the nurse and smiled. 'Alice! Where have you been, darling?'

Annie looked over at Craig and mouthed *wife*, and he nodded in understanding. Bill thought his dead wife had just walked into the room.

'Look what I have for you,' Michelle said, shaking a little cup. 'It's some sweeties for you. Hold out your hand.' She was holding a plastic cup of water in the other hand.

Bill smiled and held out a hand as if she was going to give him some gold coins. She poured the three pills into his hand, and then gave him the water when she saw him put the pills into his mouth. He swallowed them.

'Good job, Bill!' Michelle said. She turned to Annie. 'If you need anything before you leave, just give me a shout.'

'Thanks, Michelle,' Annie said.

'See you after work, Alice,' Bill said.

Michelle smiled and waved as she left the room.

'That's my Alice,' Bill said.

Craig stood up and looked at Bill. 'Was Stephen Colby innocent, Bill?' he asked bluntly.

Bill looked up at him. 'That's what I've been saying. Don't you listen? I put him away.' Bill chuckled. 'Serves the bastard right.'

'What did he do to you?' Craig said.

Then Bill yawned. 'I'm tired.'

Annie stood up. 'We'll let you get some rest,' she said.

Bill got up from his chair and lay down on his bed, while Annie and Craig said goodbye.

'You two off already?' Garfield said when he saw them come out into the hallway.

'Bill's tired,' Annie said.

'He gets that way now. If you want to give me a cigarette, I'll pass it along to him later.'

'Nice try. Go and con somebody else into giving you a ciggie.'

'I can see I'm going to have to tap Jimmy for a smoke,' Garfield said.

'I don't smoke, pal,' Craig said.

'What's the world coming to?'

'Sucks to be you,' Annie said, laughing.

EIGHTEEN

Thursday evening at the golf club in Dunfermline was quiz night, and the lounge was busy. Craig and Annie got a table for four, and waved Bailey and Biggie over.

'There's the big fella,' Bailey said, although at six-six, he literally looked down on Craig.

Craig stood up and shook their hands. 'How you been?'

'The last couple of weeks have been quiet. Just one fatal stabbing to deal with, but we have our suspect in our sights. How about you?'

'Working some cold cases.'

Bailey turned to Biggie. 'Don't just stand there looking like a lemon, get up to the bar.'

'What are you having?' Biggie said. 'Uncle Tom has the expense account, so you can have what you want.'

'Pint of lager, thanks,' Craig said.

'Usual for me, son,' Bailey said.

'A cocktail with an umbrella?' Biggie said.

'You know where that umbrella will be going if you come back with a Mai Tai. And get me a bag of pork scratchings if they have any. Crisps if they don't.'

'Aye-aye, captain.'

'Come on, I'll help you,' Annie said, and she and Biggie went to the bar.

'Is a quiz night your thing then, Jimmy?' Bailey said as they sat down.

'I haven't been to one in ages. We don't usually go out drinking during the week.'

'Me neither. I like to have a good kick at it on the weekends, though. Not going to lie, my liver takes a battering.'

Craig laughed. 'I enjoy a glass of wine after dinner. My estranged wife likes wine too.'

'So it's official then, pal? Your marriage is dead in the water?'

'You can tell?' Craig said.

'Well, if it isn't, she's very tolerant, letting Annie sleep over at your place.'

Craig nodded. 'Aye, she lives near the State Hospital, where our son is. She wanted me to go and live there, but it's not something I can do. We just couldn't agree, and so she threw twenty-five years of marriage out the window.'

'Sorry to hear that. But at least now you're wenching Annie. She's a good 'un. Salt of the earth, letting us crash at her place.'

'You helped save her life. That bastard was stalking her and he wasn't going to give up.'

'He's given up now, though, hasn't he?' Bailey said, grinning.

'Aye, he'll be going down for a long time for murder.

'Can we play in the quiz?' Annie said, bringing the drinks over with Biggie. She looked at Bailey. 'I get to do what I want since it's my birthday.'

Bailey nodded. 'Me and the lad chipped in to get you a birthday gift. Jimmy told me before we came up. Don't let me forget to give it to you before we leave.'

'Did you break the ten-shilling note?' Annie said, grinning.

'No, no, that's still in me wallet. And he's getting

a kick in the nuts before we leave,' Bailey said, nodding to Biggie.

Craig had talked to Annie before they came to the golf club, and she'd said it was okay if they talked shop regarding her uncle.

'Before they start the questions, I wanted to run something past you,' Craig said.

'Fire away, lad,' Bailey said, supping his pint.

'Annie's uncle is in a nursing home. He has dementia, and he's started talking about there being a killer in the home. Albert Fish, who was an American serial killer who died in the thirties. But he's also started talking about a killer he put away in the State Hospital thirty years ago, Stephen Colby. They suspected this guy was a serial killer. They found an ear in a trunk in his attic, along with clothing belonging to five other missing women. Six were reported missing in total, but the only thing found that suggested he killed them was the ear. Bill admitted that he fitted Colby up.'

'As much as we can believe that,' Annie said. 'He's started having periods of lucidity recently.'

'What would be the reason behind that?' Bailey asked. 'Fitting Colby up?'

'Colby had been arrested and charged with attacking Bill's son, Martin. Because Martin couldn't positively identify Colby as his attacker, Colby's case was not proven and he walked. The only witnesses who saw anything were in the pub beforehand, when Martin and Colby were arguing.'

'You think your uncle got revenge on Colby?' Biggie asked.

'I'm not sure,' Annie said. 'His mind is in and out right now, but sometimes patients like him will have bursts of clarity. That's when he started talking about a killer being in the home.'

'Annie told me about it,' Craig said, 'and we went along earlier. I would have put his rantings down to the dementia, but after he spoke to Annie about Colby, I went to speak with Colby and I have to tell you, I think there's a fifty-fifty chance that Colby is innocent. He told us what happened, and you know how you get that gut feeling?'

Bailey nodded, confirming that he did indeed know that feeling.

'And we all know prison is full of guys who say they're innocent, but today, Uncle Bill told us he'd fitted Colby up,' Annie said.

'That wouldn't hold up in court, though, would it?' Bailey said.

Craig shook his head. 'No, it wouldn't. But if he

is innocent, we have to do something to try and get him out of there.'

'Agreed. But also, if you think that Bill's talking sense about Colby, then you have to wonder if he's talking sense about a killer being in the home.'

'That went through my mind too. But that's enough shop talk. Let's play some trivia.'

NINETEEN

Eve Craig drove her car slowly down the street where she had lived for a short time after moving up from London with her husband. She had got rid of her Volvo, thinking it was an unnecessary expense, and had bought a second-hand runabout that still got her where she needed to be.

She looked at the house. The automatic timers had turned on some lights in the upstairs living room. The darkness had come down quickly, and now, just before ten p.m., it was fully dark.

She hadn't been sure she would make the trip up tonight to see him, and had even felt nervous. Seeing her husband after being married to him for twenty-five years shouldn't make her nervous, but in the past few months, they had said some harsh things to each other, and any hope she'd had of him leaving the police and coming down to live with her had been snuffed out pretty quickly.

She had bought a bottle of wine – the good stuff – and had imagined sitting with him, chatting over a few glasses, and maybe going through to the bedroom. She was dating Chris Ward, but that wasn't serious. The man was clingy and didn't have the class that her husband had.

'Jesus, Eve, you keep calling him your husband, but you've signed the separation papers,' she said out loud, talking over the DJ who was playing some music. She'd turned it down to a level where it was just background noise.

The view over to the lit-up bridges was spectacular, and she missed that. Her flat had a view of other flats across the road. Carnwath was a tiny place, with the local pub being the only source of entertainment, and then it was on to Glasgow if you wanted some serious fun. Bars, pizza places, even axe-throwing places. There had been some times when she thought about throwing an axe at Jimmy, but you could let off steam at one of those places without killing somebody with one. Although she imagined the way some people threw them, it was an accident waiting to happen.

She had questioned whether she was doing the right thing by divorcing Jimmy. She had been angry at the time and wanted her own way, and when she didn't get it, she'd acted like a spoilt child and thrown her marriage away in the process. Living on her own again after all this time was a mistake. As was having Ward round. People were allowed to make mistakes, weren't they? And everybody deserved a second chance. Jimmy would see that, wouldn't he? They could sit down like adults and come up with a solution.

She wished they had never moved from London.

Joe had been at university, but unbeknownst to them, had jacked it in. They wouldn't have found out until the three years were up, and then she supposed he would have told them. But they found out he was a serial killer, spurred on by somebody else, and that had been the end of his life. And to find out he had a dissociative disorder, well, that explained why he could kill so easily, but it would keep him in the hospital for the rest of his life.

Eve saw headlights coming round the corner further down and heading up the hill to the house. She had parked in a little layby near the house, used by dog walkers who wanted to walk along this part of the Fife coastal path. Anyone seeing her car would think it was a visitor's.

The car approached and she ducked down in her seat. It was a little Audi and it pulled into the short driveway in front of the garage. It was a car she didn't recognise. The lights turned off, and Jimmy stepped out of the passenger side, and a woman got out from the driver's side. She was laughing and walked round the front of the car and stopped to kiss Jimmy. She put her arms around his neck and pulled him closer. He wasn't fighting her off, but enjoying it.

Then they went inside and Eve saw Finn at the door.

She knew she had no right to feel angry or betrayed or anything like that, but she couldn't deny that it hurt. And seeing Finn made her cry. Her fur baby was missing his mummy, she was sure.

She saw Jimmy cross over to the curtains in the living room and was sure he looked down and saw her.

After he drew the curtains, she drove away, tears rolling down her face.

TWENTY

Craig was standing at the window, about to draw the curtains, when he looked down into the street and saw somebody sitting slumped down in the driver's seat of a car in the layby. As a copper, he was always suspicious, and tonight was no exception, even though he'd had a few drinks. Annie was sober, having just had soft drinks so she could drive him home. He'd offered to do it the other way round so she could have a drink, but she wanted him to be able to enjoy a few drinks with the boys from Yorkshire.

He wondered who this person sitting in the car was. Then the face moved and the light hit it in just the right way so he could make out who it was.

Eve.

He closed the curtains.

Christ, was she going to come in here? He hoped not. She couldn't have missed Annie kissing him on the doorstep. Craig didn't normally like a public show of affection like that, but the barriers of sobriety had been well and truly knocked down, and he enjoyed kissing her.

Eve would have had a front row seat to the display. *Shit.* Should he tell Annie? No. He didn't want to ruin her birthday. If Eve started something, then Annie would jump in. That was the last thing he wanted. If Eve came to the door, he would turn her away and tell Annie that his estranged wife just wanted to talk to him in person about...what? Their son? Her new boyfriend? He didn't know for sure that she had one, but he'd surmised it. Or maybe not. Maybe she was content to just be near Joe.

Then he heard the car start up and take off.

'Everything okay?' Annie said, coming into the room with two glasses of wine. Finn came in behind her. Craig had let him out for a pee in the back garden when they got in, and now he was settled with a ball. He lay down.

'Bloody curtains. I can never quite get them together without a slight break between them.'

'Who's going to see us from out there?' she said, smiling and setting the glasses down.

You'd be surprised. 'Just me being paranoid. There might be a bloke in Edinburgh with a powerful telescope looking across the sea, watching what we're doing.' *Or my wife might be sitting outside in a car I don't recognise.*

'Come and sit beside me,' she said.

'In a minute. I have something for your birthday.'

'I bet you do,' she said, grinning at him.

He left the room and went into his home office, where his dog-sitter, Heather, sat and used her laptop to write her books.

'I just have to get some papers together,' he shouted through.

Max Hold had shot him off a text saying he had sent some papers through to his home fax machine. He was aware that a lot of younger people sent documents through apps on their phones, then printed them off, but Craig preferred things this way. People lived on their phones, but what happened when they lost them or they got nicked?

He took the papers from the machine and took his phone out to call Max. He wondered whether he should call Eve or not. If she was going to drive home, then it would take her forty-five minutes or more, and he didn't want her driving upset. Or worse, angry.

He used his thumb to navigate to Max's number.

'Thanks for sending those papers over, son.'

'No problem, boss. I had Isla help me. They're a matter of public record; it was just making sure we found them all. Once you look at the names, then you can access our system to look at the criminal records.'

'Brilliant. I appreciate you doing that. See you tomorrow.'

'No problem, boss.'

Craig hung up and took the papers through to the living room. He was feeling a little buzzed after having a few pints and a few whiskies, but he wasn't falling down.

Christ, he said to himself, turning back to the office, where Annie's gift was sitting in a desk drawer. He took it out: a long, slim box, neatly wrapped with a sticky bow on top, and a card.

He went back through to the living room and sat down beside her. 'Happy birthday,' he said, kissing her and handing her the card and the box.

'Thank you, sweetheart,' she said, opening the card. On the front were two cartoon dogs. He hadn't wanted anything too smooshy.

She put the card down on the coffee table next to her wine glass and held the box up. 'I hope this isn't...?' She raised her eyebrows at him.

'What?'

'You know...something that buzzes.'

'An electric toothbrush? No.'

She pulled off the bow and playfully tossed it at him. Then unwrapped the box to reveal a long jewellery box. She opened it and inside was a gold chain.

'Oh, Jimmy, it's beautiful. Thank you so much.' She kissed him. 'Put it on me.'

He took the chain out and his sausage fingers fiddled with the clasp. *Fucking thing,* he said to himself. 'Listen, maybe put it on tomorrow, when I can see a bit better.'

She laughed. 'Okay. But it's fantastic.' She sipped her wine and looked at the papers he had put on the table. 'What are those? Or is it something personal?'

'It's sort of personal, for you. It's cases your uncle worked on.'

Her eyebrows went up. 'Interesting.'

'I had Max fax them over. I was just curious what murder cases your uncle worked on. And other serious cases, like rape and serious assault.'

'Can I have a look too?' Annie asked, putting the box on the table.

'Of course. They're a matter of public record.'

They split the papers up, Craig looking at the cases from thirty years ago and working towards the late nineties, early two thousands.

'He put a lot of men away,' Annie said. 'Women too.'

'He also had a lot of cases where the verdict was not proven.' Craig flipped through some more pages. 'I meant to ask you, does anybody else go in and visit your uncle?'

Annie looked at him. 'Yes. His old friend, Toby Medford. He's a retired Queen's Counsel.'

'A solicitor? Who represented criminals in court? Maybe we should cross-reference their cases.'

Annie smiled but shook her head. 'Unless you can do a search online to find the cases Toby worked on, I don't think you would be privy to that information.'

'True. But if we just narrow it down to the ones where the accused walked out of court a free man, then maybe some of those would show up.'

'Let's do that tomorrow. I'd like some alone time with James Craig, and I want his full attention.'

Craig put the papers down on the table and tried not to think of his estranged wife driving away from their house.

TWENTY-ONE

It was Roger Hammond's birthday and he wasn't happy about it. Annie Keller had been born on Roger's fifteenth birthday, but they had never met each other.

He wasn't happy with life in general and hadn't been for a long time now, but today the clock had ticked round to the first of August, and that meant he had turned sixty in his sleep. One thing he was grateful for was waking up, but now that his fifties had passed the baton to his sixties, that meant kicking it into high gear when he thought about his health.

He had woken up that morning, the sun streaming through his bedroom window, on what should have been a joyous occasion, but he'd felt nothing but depression.

No woman in his life as he entered a new era. Except for the one who was in the kitchen cooking his dinner. The smell wafted through to his nose and it made his stomach grumble.

His wife had left him, telling him he was a fat bastard, even though the scales told him he had lost a pound just the week before she left him for the postman. Apparently, the man had been delivering more than just the bills and junk mail.

If he had been younger, fitter – the diabetes wasn't all his fault; his wife liked the cream buns too – had more energy and could be bothered getting out of his armchair, he might have been more inclined to smack the postman. Roger didn't think it was worth it. Why bother losing sleep over being with somebody who didn't want to be with you?

His daughter had called first thing. The older one, the good daughter. Rita. She had attended university, got a good degree and was working in a company where she could climb the ladder. He had told her she should have joined the fire service, where she could also have climbed the ladder, but she had just looked blankly at him. Humour wasn't in her DNA. *That* she got from her mother.

His other daughter would call that evening, he was sure. Rosie. The messed-up daughter. She would call with the promise of a gift, something that she was waiting for Amazon to deliver. Apparently, they had an Amazon in Outer Mongolia and that was where his fictitious present was waiting to be shipped from.

Roger loved Rosie, of course he did, but she was seeing some arsehole who could only be described as a hippie. Long hair both on his head and on his face. Roger was sure he'd seen the beard move on its own like something was living in it. The hippie was ten years older than Rosie and had been sitting on the couch when he had first been introduced to Roger. He had called him *man*, and Roger could tell his brain was ticking away behind the veil covering the inside of his eyes. He had put his arm around Rosie as they sat on the couch, as if he was silently telling Roger she was his now. Roger had smiled, but it wasn't a smile of satisfaction from knowing his daughter was being taken care of; it was a smile of, *You don't know who you're fucking with.*

He had declined the offer of a beer and told the hippie he had to be going. The man had struggled to his feet and held out a hand for Roger to shake, which he did. It had been a power play then, with the hippie squeezing hard, but Roger had learned a trick a long time ago. A friend had told him that if somebody was squeezing a handshake, trying to break his hand, he should just stick his index and middle fingers up the inside of their wrist and they could squeeze all night with no effect.

Roger did this. Then he pulled the man close, as if going in for an embrace, and whispered in his ear, *If you touch my daughter, I'll take you apart piece by piece.*

As he pulled away, he looked the hippie in the eye, and the man could tell Roger meant it.

To this day, Roger hadn't heard from the man, and hadn't had a phone call in the middle of the night from a tearful Rosie saying the bastard had hit her.

When he got the phone call that night from Rosie, there wouldn't be any shouts from the background, the hippie wishing him happy birthday.

Roger went through to the bathroom and washed up in the sink, forgoing a shower once again. He made sure to liberally use the body spray his mother always bought for him, her silent way of telling him he was a smelly bastard.

It hadn't been his first choice, moving in with his mother, but he and his wife had had to sell their house. They'd split the proceeds, and he'd ended up with a tidy sum, enough to keep him going. He'd had a real job, fixing computers and printers and the like, and although the pay was good and had netted him a decent enough pension, he was let go because of the accusation.

'Happy birthday, teddy bear,' his mother said, putting the plate of ham steak and baked beans down in front of him at the dining table.

This mobile home was a double-wide, with three bedrooms and space in the living room for a large dining table.

'Thanks, Ma,' he replied, inwardly cringing at her use of her nickname for him. But she was touching eighty now, and he felt he couldn't criticise her, so he just smiled and tensed as she leant over to give him a kiss.

'I have a surprise for you,' she said.

'You shouldn't have,' he said, hoping it was money, although the old woman didn't have much. Maybe a twenty for him to buy some beer. He drank in the house these days, due to his having no friends. His wife hadn't wanted him to go out and get blootered with the couple of guys he hung out with, just in case some woman came on to him. The two guys had gradually faded away until he had nobody.

Then his wife had gone, doing exactly the thing she didn't want *him* to do.

His mother shuffled off and came back a few minutes later with what was obviously a bottle wrapped in leftover Christmas paper.

'Oh, what could this be?' he said, smiling at her and hoping it wasn't a bottle of supermarket cola.

He roughly tore the paper off to reveal a bottle of supermarket whisky. 'Thanks, Ma!' he said, and genuinely meant it. This would get him pished just like any other whisky, even if it didn't taste as good.

'And I have another surprise for you,' she said, heading off again, and coming back with an envelope. She passed it over and sat down opposite him.

He tore the envelope open and opened the card, revealing a ten-pound note and the words 'Happy Anniversary'. Her eyesight wasn't what it used to be, and he hoped she hadn't thought she had put in a fifty note but had mistaken it for a tenner.

'You can buy some new underwear with that,' she said with a smile.

On what planet? he thought, but smiled anyway. Buying new underwear was the last thing on his mind. Maybe he'd buy a new knife since he had lost his last one. The silly bitch had not only screamed but knocked his knife out of his hand, and it was still there, on the beach somewhere, with his prints and DNA on it, and the woman had given a good description of it. Nobody had found the fucking thing, and Roger needed to find it himself, or else he'd be locked up in a little concrete room with a man who had more than just being friends on his mind.

He knew he would have to do a clothes run soon, though. He frequented charity shops. He'd buy a sweater for the cold weather way in advance, so some nosy old woman wouldn't say to a copper, 'Oh yes, I remember selling that type of sweater to a dashingly handsome young man. I remember thinking what a twat he would look wearing a sweater with gnomes on it.' That was all he needed. But he didn't buy any ridiculous Christmas sweater, just some plain old synthetic one – never wool; wool made his skin itch like it was on fire. Then he would go to another charity shop. Always in Edinburgh, nothing local. He would buy trousers, and shoes, the latter a size or two bigger than his size. But he never, ever bought used underwear. Jesus. He imagined picking up a pair that had a brown streak in the back and a hole blown out of them. He admitted that was probably his imagination running away with itself, but still. The thought gave him the boak.

Then he would put his haul into a black bag and keep it in his attic. Which might be a problem now since his mother didn't have one, but he'd cross that bridge. There were several sheds on the property, none of which Ma was fit enough to go into.

The clothes and shoes would remain unused for months. Perfect as a disguise. He never wore any clothes he bought in a regular shop. Those modern places had cameras at the tills. Actually, for all he knew, so might the charity shop ones – but the law would hardly go around charity shops. He'd read about those muppets who went into a big DIY store and bought a murder kit – plastic sheet, duct tape, shovel and sometimes a petrol can – and they wondered how they got caught.

No, Roger was meticulous. He would wear the stuff, then dump it all miles away, and not in the one bin! The clothes would be washed first, the shoes scrubbed and bleached, then they would be cut into pieces and dumped all over creation.

It had kept him out of prison so far. But that woman screaming and knocking the knife out of his hand had almost got him caught.

It was the knife that would hang him if somebody found it and some snooping copper decided to run the prints on it because it was found at the scene of the attack.

He finished his dinner and told his mother he was going to the church later where he volunteered, sorting out clothes for the homeless and the like. He'd even given some thought to nicking some of it, but that was too risky. All it would take was some nosy cow asking why he was chorying it, and he'd have to take care of her too.

'You're such a good boy,' his mother said. 'That bitch didn't deserve you.'

'I know she didn't, Ma. I gave her the best days of my life.'

'You did.' Ma picked up a cup of tea and sipped it. Roger hoped she didn't have too much, or she'd be getting up through the night for a pee again, disturbing his sleep.

They watched TV for a while, and then Roger went to his room, telling her he was having an early night, though he was, in fact, waiting for the darkness to fall so he could go out.

There was always a risk that one of the neighbours would see him, but they were a bunch of losers. Kenny across the way was a drunk; Sylvia down the road was always entertaining men, so she kept her curtains closed most of the time; and then there was Betty, who he was sure was practising witchcraft. He didn't speak to any of the others. Bunch of tossers.

After his ma had gone around doing God knows what, he got dressed in the clothes he'd brought in from a shed earlier and went round checking the cooker knobs were turned off. Then he slipped out into the dark. He'd park somewhere and put on the wig. And the false moustache, which wouldn't pass muster in the daylight, but would certainly do its duty in the dark.

He drove along to Aberdour and went down to the beach. He would have a look for the knife, and then if anybody was here, he might scout out the place, see if she was alone or had a big radge dog with her. One time he had approached a lone woman who was sitting with her German Shepherd. The fucker had a set of teeth on him, that was for sure, and Roger had nearly blown a hole in the back of his own drawers. Thinking quickly on his feet, he'd asked her if she had seen a little poodle running loose. She had told him no, and hoped he found little Lulu. Roger had walked away, quickly turning his back on her, and felt like a real twat as he started shouting for the fictitious Lulu.

There was another car in the car park, just one.

He turned his car, making sure the headlights illuminated the inside of the other one. There might be a young couple in the back, but if there was, they would have to be very agile as it was a small car.

Sure it was empty, he stopped, turned off the engine and killed the lights. He slipped on the wig and the mock facial hair, using his phone camera to check them. The wig looked okay, not perfect, but he wasn't going for an interview to be a circus clown.

He made sure the interior light switch was off before opening the door, and he took the walking stick out from the back and started walking with a limp through the car park towards the beach.

It was deserted. Except for a figure near the public toilets. He started walking along towards the building. There were two toilet pods outside the building, but Roger never used them. He was paranoid about getting stuck inside and having to call somebody to get him out. He wondered if he could flush the wig down the toilet if that situation arose, but that might have them asking more questions than he needed.

The sky was dark, but there was a summer tint to it – unlike the winter sky, when it was darker than a coal miner's arsehole. The closer he got to the figure, the more he could make it out, and he saw it was a woman. Not a young thing, but he didn't want them too young. Now he was sixty, one of them might overwhelm him and give him a kicking.

He had a knife in his pocket, the stab-o-matic number two. His own name for the knife. If this woman was somebody he could count on as being his next victim, he would forget about his first partner in crime, keeping his fingers crossed that the elements would take care of any of his DNA on it. If indeed there was any. He just couldn't be sure. He was ninety-nine per cent sure he had worn gloves that night, but it was always the one per cent that could hang you.

The closer he got, the more excited he felt. The ski mask was in his pocket, ready to whip on. The wig and tash were just in case – God forbid – it was somebody who recognised him and then managed to evade him. He wasn't exactly an athlete now and running after them was out of the question. It was his knees that gave him problems, and he was almost sure he had a heart condition, but without a doctor poking and probing him and possibly shoving a camera up his dingdong, he could only go by how out of breath he got.

He didn't recognise the woman. She sat down on a bench, her back to him. He stopped and looked around for Fido – or even worse, Thor – but there was no sign of a dog.

Roger managed to get up close to her and stopped, taking the ski mask out and putting it on. It wasn't a tight fit with the wig on, and by Christ he had forgotten to take off the tache in his haste and now the fucking thing was inside the woollen helmet doing its own thing, covering part of his mouth. The bloody thing tickled his face and he almost aborted this mission, but what if she suddenly turned round and saw only his eyes and his mouth with a hairy caterpillar half-covering it? No, he had to carry on.

He took a step forward and reached her, his hand in his pocket grasping the knife.

Suddenly, she stood and turned to face him. But it wasn't a woman. It was a man. Wearing a better wig than his.

'Hello, Roger,' he said, taking the wig off. 'Is this what you're looking for?' He held up Roger's knife. The one he'd lost on the beach. Stab-o-matic number one.

Roger's legs were shaking. *He knows my name,* he thought. *He has my knife. Who is this man?*

Then things took a turn he didn't see coming.

'It's my birthday,' Roger said, but there would be no cake, no party. No fun stuff. Just bloodshed.

TWENTY-TWO

Craig's doorbell rang, and Finn went off his nut, running downstairs in the hope of clenching his jaws around a bawbag or two.

Annie was in the kitchen making breakfast.

'Finn!' Craig shouted, but the dog was well ahead of him, raging at the door now. Craig quickly checked the footage from his Ring doorbell and saw it was the boys from Yorkshire. He opened the door.

'Tom, Biggie. Come away in.'

Finn was excited when he sensed there was no threat, and both of the visitors petted him before he ran away upstairs.

'Thanks, lad,' Bailey said, leading the way.

Biggie followed. 'Thanks, sir,' he said.

'This house has an inverted layout,' Craig said.

'The living room and kitchen are upstairs. Just follow the dog.' He closed the front door, after having a quick look to make sure Eve wasn't parked outside again.

Upstairs, Annie came out from the kitchen and smiled at the detectives. 'Hello, boys. Hungry?'

'I am, but I can't believe he's got you slaving away in the kitchen,' Bailey said.

She leaned in close. 'Don't worry, I'll have him take me to an expensive restaurant to make up for it. But to be honest, he did offer.'

'That's my girl.' He handed over his present. 'It's nowt, really. Open it later.'

'I have something for you too,' Biggie said, bringing out a small box.

'What? You going to get down on one knee now? I think Jimmy might have something to say about that,' Bailey said.

'Give over,' Biggie said.

Finn looked at Biggie like he was asking where his gift was.

'Go get your ball,' Craig told him. The dog ran into the living room, where he started barking. 'Heather, the dog-sitter, should be here in a little while,' he told the men.

'Champion,' Bailey said. 'Let us give you a hand

with those plates, love,' he said as Annie started dishing out the full Scottish.

'That would be great. I made coffee in the percolator.'

'This all smells wonderful. I appreciate you doing this for us,' Bailey said.

'Yeah, thanks, Annie,' Biggie said.

After they'd eaten breakfast, Craig sat them down in the living room and showed them the papers. 'Court cases that Annie's uncle presided over.'

Bailey took some sheets and leafed through them. 'You think he was fixing some of the cases?' He looked at Annie. 'No offence.'

'None taken. But not necessarily fixing them. It's just that there seems to be a lot of cases that ended up being not proven, that uniquely Scottish verdict.'

'Aye, we don't have that down south,' Biggie said.

'We're going to look into it further,' Craig said.

Just then, Heather turned up.

'Gentlemen, this is Heather, who looks after Finn for me. But I'm on borrowed time as she's becoming a bestselling author.'

'How do,' Bailey said.

'Pleased to meet you,' Biggie said.

'Bestselling author, eh?' Bailey said. 'I'm impressed.'

Heather's cheeks got sudden sunburn. 'Not exactly bestselling. I'm working on that. I self-publish on Amazon.'

'Good for you, lass. Open up your phone and let me and the lad see your books.'

'Just three right now, but I'm working on book four in my detective series.'

She opened her phone and showed them her books.

'I'll buy them later and give them five stars,' Biggie said.

'That's very kind,' Heather said.

'No problem, lass. Just make sure he pays you well for looking after the boy.' He put a hand at the side of his mouth and whispered, 'Scottish people.'

'I'm Scottish,' Heather said, smiling.

'Present company excepted.'

'Right, before you slag me off anymore, we should be hitting the road,' Craig said. Then to Heather: 'These two are getting commendations.'

'Nice. Well deserved, from what I heard.'

'You're trying to make a Yorkshireman blush,' Bailey said. 'It won't happen. *He* might blush, because he's a southern git.'

'You're hilarious, boss,' Biggie said.

'Thanks for taking care of my boy,' Craig said to Heather. 'If anybody comes by, don't let him go with them. Please call me if that happens.'

'I will, but who...?'

'Anybody. Catch you later.'

Both Heather and Finn looked puzzled as he left.

TWENTY-THREE

Jimmy was in his office while the Yorkshire lads were in the conference room getting their commendations. He was going through paperwork when his phone rang.

'Hello?'

'Jimmy?'

'Speaking.'

'It's Harry McNeil.'

'Hey, pal, how's it going?'

'I've had quieter Fridays. I just had a call from our mortuary over here. Finbar O'Toole, to be precise.'

'How's he doing?' Craig said. Finbar had helped talk to Annie's ex-husband when they thought he was stalking her.

'Fine, but he wanted me to know about the two decomposing bodies that were found.'

'Two? We only had one,' Craig said.

'That's the thing; we had one too, found in a cemetery. The bushes were cut back, revealing the body. Like somebody had deliberately revealed him.'

'That's similar to our find. The dead man was sitting in a chair in a house when the council went round to evict the tenant. Like he had been killed somewhere else and then brought back to the house.'

'And another thing, Jimmy: Finbar said that both bodies had been mutilated. Both of them had had their genitals cut off in almost the exact same manner.'

'Jesus,' Craig said. 'Any luck with identification?'

'Not with ours. Yours had ID on him, but his identity still has to be confirmed. But the way they were killed is almost identical. Like they were killed by the same person,' Harry said.

'I had one of my boys do a background on the name we have. He was a real bad bastard. A rapist who walked out of court a free man.'

'Christ. Who screwed that one up?'

'Before my time, mate. Somebody dropped the ball, though.'

'Right, Jimmy, I'll keep you in the loop. If we get an ID on ours, I'll give you a call.'

'Great stuff. You still coming over to the party tomorrow night?'

'We'll all be there – Finbar, Stewart and myself. Alex is away on a job with McGovern just now, so it's just going to be the three of us, like a bunch of sad bastards who can't get a woman.'

Craig laughed. 'We'll look forward to seeing you lot anyway.'

'See you tomorrow, my friend.'

Harry hung up and Craig went back to his computer screen. He read through Eddie Hay's record. The man had been an animal. He had been accused of raping two women, but when he got to court, one of them was dead and the other one couldn't convince the jury of his guilt. His verdict had been not proven.

He looked at the surviving victim's name: Suzie Carr.

The missing woman who Stephen Colby had said was still alive.

He got up and walked into the incident room, and pulled up an office chair next to Isla.

'Do you remember the name that Stephen Colby

gave us? The woman he was accused of murdering after they found some of her clothing in his attic?'

'I do; he said her name was Suzie Carr.'

'Correct. The corpse we found yesterday in Leven, Eddie Hay? He was accused of raping Suzie, but he walked. He was actually accused of raping two women, but one of them was dead by the time it went to court. Then it was his word against Suzie's, and they made mincemeat of her.'

'Then she disappeared,' Isla said.

'She was reported missing and never heard from again.'

'And Hay was spoken to about this?' Isla asked.

'There's no record of it. Maybe they didn't want a lawsuit for harassment. Whatever the reason, there's no record of him being interviewed.'

'What did Colby say about Suzie Carr again?' Isla asked.

'He said she was a nurse who came to the State Hospital one day. He only saw her once, but he was in no doubt it was her.'

'How did he know her? How could he be so sure?'

'I looked at her missing person report, and it says Suzie was a nurse in Dunfermline when she was raped. Stephen Colby was a male nurse. He worked beside her for a short time.'

'So he knew her, and then he got locked up for murdering her and other women. But then, supposedly, she turned up at the State Hospital one day and he recognised her.' Isla looked at Craig. 'If that's true, then there would be a record of her being at the hospital.'

'Unless she changed her name.'

'Christ, yes,' Isla said. 'We could always check the court records. She'd have had to petition to change her name.'

'Let's get onto that. I mean, you can do that.'

'I'll make a call. It might take some time for somebody to find the info and give it to us.'

'Thanks, Isla.'

Craig went back into his office and sat down, pulling up Suzie Carr's file again. He wanted to go over her witness statement.

He started reading.

TWENTY-FOUR

Suzie's story

It was a week before Christmas and I had picked up a few more shifts at the hospital. There seemed to be a bit of flu going around and some of the staff had called out. I needed the money, to buy gifts for my nieces and nephews, and they were glad to have anybody who wanted to work late or come in on a day off.

I remember it was snowing that week. Big, wet, slushy stuff that stuck to the ground. Buses were having a hard time getting around and the gritters couldn't keep up with the snowfall.

I had finished my shift at three that afternoon

and they asked me if I could do an overnight. I went home and went to bed for a while. Then I got up, showered and had something to eat. It was still snowing heavily outside. I didn't have a car, and I tried getting a taxi, but they were so busy, the wait was an hour.

I decided to start walking and hoped I would see a bus coming. I made it to the bus stop. The snow was coming down thick and fast. Cars were getting up and down the road but going slowly.

The bus stop was outside the entrance to a park, and I remember thinking how nice and pretty it looked, like a Christmas card. I turned to look back down the street to see if I could see a bus coming, and that's when I felt a hand come round my head and go over my mouth. I felt myself being yanked backwards off my feet. I kicked and tried to scream, but it was slippery, and I couldn't scream because of his hand.

He dragged me into the park and pulled me behind some bushes. He threw me down onto the ground, which didn't hurt because I landed on my side. He stomped on my stomach, knocking the wind out of me. Then he leaned down. He was wearing a ski mask, so I couldn't see his features, but as soon as he spoke, I knew it was him. I could smell the stink of his breath, he was so close. He lay down on top of me after pulling my trousers and pants down, and then he raped me.

Afterwards, he left me undressed in the snow and he walked towards the gate of the park. He took his ski mask off and that's when I saw him. I saw him clearly.

I got dressed, the snow falling on me. I felt scared, humiliated, and thought he might come back to kill me. He'd said he would kill me if I made a sound.

I walked home after that. I was too scared to call the police then. As a nurse, I should have known better, but I just couldn't.

Later on, I reported it to the police.

TWENTY-FIVE

Craig sat back in his chair and thought about the torment Suzie Carr had gone through. Being raped by some filthy bastard who had gone on to be accused of raping another woman, but then escaped justice.

And now somebody had killed him and left him sitting in a chair in his house. Killed him in the same manner as the victim who had been found in Warriston Cemetery.

He would wait and see if they could get an approximate date of when Hay had died. Then they could have Suzie Carr in for an interview.

He saw Bailey and Biggie come into the incident room and got up to go and speak to them. 'How did it go?'

'The boss said drinks are on you all weekend, chief. His words, not mine,' Bailey said. 'Isn't that right, short stack?'

'Don't bring me into your evil ways,' Biggie said. The younger detective looked at Craig. 'You have to excuse him, sir. I think the congratulary handshake went to his head.'

'Right, that's enough talking shite now,' Bailey said.

'Don't worry, pal, it's a free bar in the private room at the golf club tomorrow,' Craig said.

'Now you're singing my tune,' Bailey said.

Dan Stevenson turned round in his chair.

'We got a shout, boss.'

'What is it?' Craig said.

'Body in a car down at Aberdour beach.'

'Right.' Craig got his jacket from his office. 'Isla. Let's go.' He looked at Bailey. 'Tag along if you like. As consultants, mind.'

'You're the boss,' Bailey said. He looked at Biggie. 'You want me to drive?'

'My car says he doesn't like Uncle Tom. I'll drive.'

'Why I've never kicked you in the bollocks before is beyond me.'

Bailey and Biggie followed Craig, Dan and Isla,

but Bailey insisted they put the address into the sat nav first as, according to him, Biggie had as much sense of direction as an apple rolling downhill.

'I got us up here to Scotland again, didn't I?' Biggie said.

'With sat nav. You just proved my point, boy.'

The car park at Aberdour beach was busy, which amounted to half a dozen cars parked. Absolutely bursting at the seams by Aberdour standards. One car sat in the far corner on its own, away from all the other cars.

Craig saw Annie's car parked away from the rest of the vehicles, the mortuary van parked further away. There was no sign of Annie. Forensics tarps had been put around what Craig assumed was the car in which the body had been found.

'I bet that's stinking inside,' Isla said.

'Depends how long he's been in there,' Dan replied.

'You were only in the car twenty minutes and *you* did a good job.' She grinned at him.

'You know, when I put in for sick leave, I'll tell them I couldn't take it anymore.'

'Big strapping lad like you? They'd never believe you,' Craig said.

'I'm being ganged up on here,' Dan said.

The Nissan SUV slowly pulled in behind Craig's car, and Bailey and Biggie got out.

'That was a laugh,' Bailey said. 'I'm sure he was a kamikaze pilot in another life. Bloody great lorry coming steaming towards us and he decides to play chicken with it. What does *bawbag* mean? Or should I just take it as read?'

'Yep, it means what you think it means,' Isla said.

'I fooking knew it. That bastard truck driver better be well on his way when we get out of here.'

'I had everything under control,' Biggie said.

'Compared to what? A burning Messerschmitt?' Bailey shook his head, then turned to the others. 'Have you had a look yet?'

'No, we just got here. Apparently, Dan's favourite film is *Driving Miss Daisy*,' Isla said.

'I think he was talking to me,' Craig said.

'I knew that.' Isla smiled at him.

'No. We can have a look now.' Craig walked over to the uniform standing a few feet away from the cordoned-off car, and he told the man about Bailey and Biggie.

'Oh, you're the detectives who got the commendation. I heard that was happening. Congratulations, sirs.' The uniform smiled at the two men from Yorkshire.

'Thanks, lad,' Bailey said. 'But we were only too happy to help out.'

'The forensics team are there,' the uniform said to Craig. 'The pathologist too. Ms Keller.'

'Thanks,' Craig said.

He walked towards the tarps leaving the others behind to talk to the uniforms, and saw Annie standing off to one side, talking on her phone. Her voice was raised, but he couldn't make out what she was saying. She saw him looking and quickly hung up.

'Look who's here!' she said, smiling.

'Is everything okay?' he asked her.

'I'm fine. It's nothing. Just my dad being an arsehole. I called him to let him know about my uncle, and he seemed his usual ambivalent self.'

'You haven't spoken to him for a long time, you said.'

'Correct. And that will be the last time.'

Stan Mackay came round from the tarp and saw Craig with Annie. 'It's a nasty one alright. From what I can see, there's a lot of blood in his groin area. But that's where I hand it over to you, Annie.'

'Any ID on him?' Craig asked.

Mackay nodded. 'A wallet. Roger Hammond's

his name. His address is at the mobile home park at Fordell, just up from Hillend.'

'Thanks, Stan,' Craig said. He called Dan over and gave him the name to run, and told him to cross-check it with the car's licence plate.

'Okay, boss.'

Annie walked over to her car, popped the boot and took out a white suit.

'This is all we need,' she said when she was suited up. 'We're busy as hell as it is.'

'Don't stress about it,' Craig said. 'Just focus on the party tomorrow night.'

'Can I smoke at it?' she asked, smiling.

'You're a grown woman; you can do what you like.'

'You're no fun. You're supposed to tell me no, I can't smoke, and then I can go off in a huff and you can make it up to me.'

'Oh, okay then...No, you can't smoke.'

'Too late.'

Another car entered the car park and slowly drove towards them. DSup Mark Baker.

'Christ, he's driving like he's pished,' Annie said.

'Was there ever a time that you liked Baker?' Craig asked.

'What? I love that wee guy. Who would I get to slag off if he wasn't around?'

'You love another man? I don't think we can carry on with our relationship.'

'Oh, shut up. You're the only man I love.' She snapped her mouth shut. 'You made me say that. I take it back. I was talking out of anger. You manipulated me, you big bastard,' she said as her face started to go red. 'I meant to say loathe. You're the only man I *loathe*.'

Craig laughed. '*Loathe* you too.'

'Oh, sod off. I'm never talking to you again.' She walked away.

Bailey walked up to Craig. 'Trouble in paradise?'

Craig shook his head. 'No, we're just having a bit of a discussion about her smoking habits.'

'Ah.' Bailey looked at Craig knowingly.

'Now here's a man who's having trouble in paradise,' Craig said, nodding towards Baker.

'Really? Do tell, son.'

'He met a younger woman online and she's a bunny boiler.'

'Oh Jesus. Is he coming to the party tomorrow?'

'He is,' Craig said.

'And we get to meet the aforementioned boiler?'

'I'm hoping so.'

'You had a look at the victim yet, Jimmy?' Mark Baker said, wandering across, looking like he had been sleeping on a park bench.

'Not yet, sir. Annie just went to have a look, then we'll have a squint at him once she's running her eyes over him. Stan Mackay said it's a bad one. Had his bollocks cut off, apparently.'

'Christ's sake. What the hell have we got going on here? A man found mutilated in a house, and now this one too.'

'And one in Edinburgh too. Harry McNeil called me. They found one in a cemetery.'

'Oh Jesus. A serial?'

'I would think so,' Craig answered, just as one of the uniforms shouted over that the pathologist was ready for them to have a look.

'Come on, son, you may as well have some input on this,' Baker said to Bailey, as he and Craig walked towards the car.

Biggie stood talking to Isla as Craig moved forward.

The car was a small hatchback, red, and stood out like a sore thumb. The windows were tinted a deep black colour. In the back seat sat a man with his head hanging to one side. In his lap was dried blood. Lots of it. His genitalia were on the floor.

'Killed in place, as you can see,' Annie said. 'Then he was stabbed in the region of his heart, but with the amount of blood loss.'

Craig turned round and saw his team standing nearby, waiting for instructions. 'Isla, ask one of the uniforms what time this was called in. When the guy was noticed in here.'

Isla nodded and went to speak with a uniform and came back a few moments later. 'Forty minutes ago. A couple of lads were looking at the car. There were other cars, just a couple, but these two boys were looking for something to nick and saw him sitting in the back. They called it in. They're being spoken to now, and statements were taken from the other people who were here.'

'This looks very personal to me,' Bailey said.

Craig nodded. 'We'll check if he has any family members or girlfriends who might have a jealous ex. Whoever did this didn't miss. His tackle's on the floor.'

'Brings the tears to me eyes, that does,' Bailey said.

Dan came back and approached Craig. 'Roger Hammond is a predator. He's got several arrest records, but nothing proved.'

'Thanks Dan.'

Craig nodded and took his phone out. 'Max. It's Craig. I need you to do a wee search for me. On our victim, Roger Hammond.'

'Sure, boss, no problem.'

Craig hung up, and they stood around talking about cases until Craig's phone rang.

'Max.'

'Hammond's a predator alright. He attacked a woman at knifepoint. But she fought back and knocked the knife out of his hand. When he went to court, it was not proven. He walked.'

'How long ago was that?' Craig asked.

'Five years ago.'

'Who was the judge presiding over the case?'

'Bill Keller.'

'Thanks, Max. Can you get me a list of victims. And the details of that woman who fought back when he attacked her.'

'I'll get Gary to get onto it right away and get back to you.'

Craig hung up. 'Bill Keller let Hammond walk free from court after a not proven verdict was returned.'

'Jesus,' Bailey said. 'Annie's uncle certainly did the rounds, didn't he? Letting those filthy bastards walk the streets again.'

'Hammond's name must be in that list I showed you last night,' Craig said.

'You told me Keller started suffering from dementia four years ago. This could have been one of the last cases he worked on.'

'I'm going back to Dunfermline to talk to him again. Why don't you come with me, Tom?'

'I can do that. Biggie, stay here and don't make an arse of yourself.'

'As if.'

'Dan, take charge here and make sure all the witness statements are on my desk later,' Craig said. He looked at Bailey. 'I'll just be one minute.'

'Take your time, chief.'

Craig walked back over to the car and slipped behind the tarp. 'I'm going to see your uncle, Annie. The victim here was accused of attacking a woman five years ago, and your uncle presided over the case. Hammond walked free.'

'What does that mean, Jimmy? You think my uncle let him walk?'

'I'm not saying that. But he did let a lot of men walk.'

'What are you going to talk to him about?'

'About his past cases. See if any daylight can get through to him.'

Annie nodded. 'Please be careful with him.'

'I will.' He smiled at her. 'You know you're the only woman I love, don't you?' He turned and walked away.

Annie smiled, then took her phone out. She was going to text Craig, but then she saw the text that had just come in. Following the phone call with the stranger. It hadn't been her dad, but obviously somebody else who hated her just as much as her father did.

Drop it. Last warning.

TWENTY-SIX

'Back so soon?' the nurse, Michelle, said as Craig and Bailey walked along the corridor in the nursing home.

'I'd like my friend to see Bill,' Craig said.

Michelle smiled at him. 'Absolutely. What's your name?'

'Tom. Call me Tom.' Bailey smiled at his own joke and Michelle chuckled.

'Tom it is. But I don't believe I caught your name the last time.'

'Jimmy,' Craig said.

'Go right in. Bill's watching TV. Give me a shout if you need anything.'

'Is Garfield not working today?' Craig asked.

'Day off. Would either of you like a cup of coffee?'

'That would be smashing, thanks,' Bailey said. 'Just milk for me. I'm sweet enough, so my wife says, but she drinks a lot, so what does she know?'

Michelle smiled at him. She was a woman in her thirties with blonde hair pulled back into a ponytail.

'Black for me, please,' Craig said. 'Thanks, Michelle.'

'No problem. I'll be right back with those.'

She walked away, and they found Bill's room. The old boy was watching a crime show on TV. Some rerun.

'Morse,' Bill said as they entered his room. 'Brilliant. Best detective there is.'

'Hi, Bill,' Craig said. 'This is my friend Tom.'

Bill looked up at Bailey, all six foot six of him staring down at the old man. 'How's the weather up there?' He chuckled.

'Pleased to meet you, Bill. I'm a detective. Like Morse.'

Bill perked up at this. 'Really? Come in, come in, shut the door.'

Craig shut the door and sat on the bed, letting Bailey sit on the small visitor's chair.

'There's a killer in here,' Bill said. 'In the home. I

saw him. I looked him right in the eye and I asked him outright if he was guilty of the crimes and he said nothing. He didn't have the balls to admit it. But I stood inches away from him.' He looked at Bailey. 'He's wandering around the home like he owns the place. Nobody stopping him or taking him to task.'

'What does he look like?' Bailey asked. 'Maybe Jimmy and I could have a word with him.'

'Average build. Average looks. Except for one distinguishing mark.'

'What would that be?' Craig asked.

'A small scar above his top lip.' Bill nodded. 'Oh yes. Nasty bastard. Looks like the sort of dirt bucket I'd throw the book at.'

'Do you know his name?' Bailey asked.

'Morse, I think.'

'Oh, right.'

Craig looked at Bill. 'Roger Hammond died.'

Bill put his head back and laughed. 'That bastard. He was a fucking menace to society. He's had that coming for a long time.' He looked away and sniggered. 'Serves the bastard right.'

'Who killed him, Bill?' Bailey asked.

Bill suddenly stopped laughing and turned to look at the big detective. 'It certainly wasn't Albert Fish. He's in here. I saw him. Nasty bastard. Got a bloody scar. He thinks that makes him hard. I'll give him hard alright. Just wait until I lock him away with all the real hard bastards.'

Bailey looked at Craig, who nodded.

'You liked being a judge, didn't you, Bill?' Craig said.

'Loved it, son. Best job I ever had. I got to see their faces as they knew they had fucked up and I was going to send them down.'

'You didn't send all of them down, though, did you?' Craig said.

Bill chuckled. 'Not all of them. Some of them got to walk free. Can you believe that? A jury thought they were innocent and they walked out of court.'

'Not innocent,' Craig said. 'You just couldn't prove they were guilty.'

'I didn't need to prove they were guilty. I *knew* they were guilty, but I had to go with what those foolish people said. It was disgusting. But they were taken care of.'

'What do you mean?' Bailey asked.

'Do you like Morse?' Bill asked.

'Can't say I watch many detective shows,' Bailey replied. 'Before Roger died, he managed to identify his attackers.'

Bill's face fell. 'What did he say?'

'That's something we can't discuss,' Bailey said.

'Did he say anything about Albert Fish?'

'No, that's not a name he gave us.'

'It wasn't Belle, was it?'

Michelle came into the room. 'Here we are, gentlemen. Two coffees.' She set them down on the hospital table at the end of the bed and smiled. 'Any biscuits? We have Jammy Dodgers or Hobnobs.'

'Nothing for me,' Bailey said.

'I'm fine, thanks,' Craig said.

'Good. Give me a shout if you need anything.' She left the room.

'Who's Belle?' Craig asked.

'I like Morse. I like his car,' Bill said, watching the TV again.

Bailey drank some of his coffee, which was surprisingly good.

'Roger says he wants to talk to you later,' Bailey said, figuring that Bill wouldn't remember that they had just told him that the man had died.

'Roger does?' Bill looked away from the TV again.

'Yes. He said he knows who hurt him and he wants to come and see you.'

'I didn't touch him. I'm in here. How could I?'

Bill smiled, but there was no humour in it. 'I want to watch some TV now. Tell Roger he can blow.'

Both detectives got up to leave.

'See you soon, Bill,' Craig said.

Bill looked at him. 'That snooping copper was round here. Be careful what you say to him if you see him. And that Nosy bitch. I can't stand her. Never could. My brother's daughter is a pain in the arse. Just watch what you say to her as well.'

'I will,' Craig said. 'Did you take care of Roger like we agreed?'

Bill laughed and nodded his head. 'Of course we did. Stupid boy. I told you we were going to. I hope he rots in hell, the dirty bastard. But never mind that; remember what I said about that copper.'

'I will.'

Bill looked at Bailey. 'Why did you dye your hair?'

Bailey thought on his feet. 'I just felt I should do that in case somebody saw me with Roger.'

'Why are you speaking funny?' Bill asked.

'It's my disguise.' Bailey leaned in closer to Bill and whispered, 'Like we talked about. The hair and the voice, remember?'

'God, yes! How could I forget? That was a good

idea. Pity you couldn't do anything about your size, fat bastard.' Bill chuckled. 'You all set for tonight?'

Bailey looked at him. 'What's happening tonight again?'

'You know. What we talked about.'

'I've forgotten.'

'Never mind. Belle will remind you. I'll talk to her later.'

'Belle?' Bailey said. 'You mean Annie?'

Bill looked horrified. 'Don't mention that bitch to me. No, I mean Belle, you idiot.'

'We haven't seen Belle for ages,' Bailey said. 'Have we, Jimmy?'

'No, we haven't. Where is she now?'

Bill put a finger to his lips. 'Walls have ears.' Then he winked and tapped the side of his nose. 'Right, you better get going. My useless son is coming in. Don't say a word. You and Belle, mum's the word.'

'Right you are. But can you remind me about tonight?'

'I had a dog once,' Bill said. Then he leaned over and whispered to Bailey, 'Who's he?'

'Just a friend of mine.'

'Your boyfriend?'

Bailey started to feel his cheeks burn, which

didn't happen very often. 'No, no, just a friend.' *Fuck.*

'Oh, right. He's an ugly bastard anyway. You can do better for yourself. Like that nurse. She's nice. We used to go out, you know.'

'She seems like a nice woman,' Bailey said.

'She is. Make sure you look after her. See you tomorrow.'

Just then, a tall man in his fifties walked in and looked at them. 'Everything okay?' he asked.

'And you are?' Craig said.

'Martin Keller, Bill's son. And you?'

'Oh, right. Sorry. I'm Jim Craig. This is my friend, Tom Bailey. We just popped in to see your dad.'

'Okay. Nice to meet you,' Keller said, shaking their hands.

'Right then, we'll be off,' Bailey said, but Bill was already watching TV again, lost in his own world.

'Don't rush on my account,' Keller said.

'We were just leaving,' Craig said, and he and Bailey filed out of the room.

Down the corridor, they met Michelle.

'That you off then?' she said.

'Yes,' Craig said. 'I think Bill is getting tired.'

'He has his ups and downs. Time to get him down for a nap, I think.'

'Thanks for the coffee,' Bailey said.

'Any time. Take care.'

She walked away, and Craig turned to watch her go and saw Garfield Clover going into Bill's room. Michelle went in after him and closed the door behind her. He was surprised at Garfield's dedication. Michelle had told him it was Garfield's day off.

Craig and Bailey walked down the stairs and out into the sunshine. They didn't start talking until they were at Craig's Volvo.

'That's the strangest conversation I've had in a long time. And that includes with me wife,' Bailey said as they got into the car.

'It's like opening curtains, then shutting them, then opening them again. But when he's saying these things, it's not as if he's making them up. We're getting a glimpse into his mind. He certainly remembers Roger Hammond.' Craig looked out the window and saw a familiar face, albeit he was dressed differently from the last time he'd seen him.

Jackson Clover was driving a black van, dressed in a black suit and wearing a black tie. Craig rolled his window down.

'Jackson.'

Jackson got out of the van and walked over. 'Hey, Jim, how's things?'

'Keeping busy, but I wanted to pop in and see Annie's uncle.'

'Old Bill. Garfield told me that Annie's uncle was here now. Big let down for him, considering he was a judge.'

'It's a shame how the mind goes,' Craig said. 'You work for an undertaker?'

'I *am* the undertaker. I own the business. Clover's Funeral Services. Garfield and I inherited it from our father. We each own it equally, but Garfield doesn't want any part of it.'

'I didn't see him today.'

'He's got the day off, but he usually works later.' Jackson looked at his watch. 'Better be off. I have several rounds to do. Including some poor old bugger in here. Heart attack, they reckon.'

'I won't keep you. See you tomorrow.'

'See ya.'

Jackson Clover went back to his van and Craig pulled away. 'I know Bill's destined for a ride in one of those vans one day, and just the thought of it upsets Annie. Her estranged father is Bill's brother.'

'She doesn't talk to her old man?' Bailey said. 'That's a sad state of affairs.'

'She was arguing with him on the phone earlier. She wasn't pleased to speak to him, that's for sure.'

'She should try and make up with the old bastard before it's too late.'

'I wonder if it would be worth inviting him along to the party. Mend some fences.'

'Do you know how to get in touch with him?'

'No, but I know somebody who can find out.' Craig pulled into the side of the road and called Max Hold, asking him to find the address for Annie's father.

TWENTY-SEVEN

Annie was back in the mortuary, dealing with the deceased when Jackson Clover walked into the receiving area pushing a metal gurney with a coffin on it.

'Hey, you,' he said to her. She turned to look at him and then smiled.

'Hi, Jackson. Keeping busy today, I see.'

'Absolutely. I just bumped into your "friend",' he said, using air quotes.

'You know he's my boyfriend. It just seems funny being in your forties and saying you have a boyfriend.'

'I know. I was like that with his nibs. Now we're married, "husband" sounds so much better.'

'It does indeed. Better than divorcee, which I

technically am. At least that sounds better than single at my age.' She stepped closer to him. 'You know DSup Mark Baker?'

'Can't say I do,' Jackson replied.

'Oh. Well, never mind then.' Annie was going to tell him about Baker's new girlfriend, but there was no point now. 'What's new with you?' she asked instead.

'Nothing much. Just working hard.'

'I know that feeling.'

'Jimmy had that bloke from Yorkshire in his car when I saw him at the home.'

'He's taken a shine to Bill,' Annie said.

'That's nice. Bill doesn't get many visitors.'

Annie smiled. 'Who are you here for today?'

Jackson reached into his pocket and pulled out the paperwork. 'Mrs McGuire. Natural causes.'

'Oh yes. No PM needed. I'll get Seth to get her out for you.'

She walked away and went looking for Seth in the PM suite, where he was preparing a sudden death for autopsy.

'Jackson Clover is here for Mrs McGuire,' she said. 'Could you get her out of the fridge for me, please?'

'No problem, boss. I'll get Drew to help me.'

Seth walked out to go and look for his friend, while Annie went back to the receiving area. Jackson wasn't there. She went to look in her office. He wasn't there either. There wasn't anywhere else down here he could have gone. Jesus. Had he gone upstairs for some reason?

Then the door to the break room opened and Jackson walked out, holding a bag of crisps and a can of cola.

'Don't tell Garfield, Annie. I'm supposed to be on a diet, but I miss my crisps and Coke. My brother thinks I'm a fat sod as it is. One day he'll get his own place and give me peace.'

She smiled at him. 'No problem. You're still coming to the party tomorrow?'

'Of course we are. Free booze and dancing with a woman just so my husband will get jealous? You bet your boots we are.'

The doors to the PM suite opened, and Drew and Seth came out.

'She's all safe and sound in the coffin,' Seth said.

'Thanks, lads. You're the salt of the earth. I'd open my bag of crisps and share them with you, but I'm a greedy bastard.'

'They're out of date anyway,' Seth said. 'I got a bag earlier and they're foosty.'

'They are? Oh, bastard things.' Jackson looked at the packet while still holding the Coke and read the date. Seth was right. 'Oh well, I've eaten worse.' He laughed and went through the doors into the receiving area, the two assistants following to help him out with the gurney.

A few minutes later, Seth and Drew came back to Annie's office, where she was on the phone with Stan Mackay.

'They're going to be a while yet with Roger Hammond in the car,' she said after finishing her call. 'More than likely, we'll store him tonight, and then we'll have to do the PM tomorrow. Sorry to have to bring you in on the weekend, but at least it's party time tomorrow night.'

'No problem,' Seth said. 'We're looking forward to it.'

'We are,' Drew agreed.

'I meant me and my girlfriend,' Seth said.

'That's what I meant,' Drew said, making a face.

'Well, if we're all done for the day, time to go home,' Annie said.

'See you first thing, boss,' Seth said. And they all left.

TWENTY-EIGHT

CASE # SL – 8729846 – C

He walked along the busy street, not making eye contact with anybody, minding his own business. He had taught this to his wife, Carla: be aware of your surroundings, but make sure you don't lock eyes with anybody.

That was what he was doing now, crossing the street every so often, stopping to look in a shop window even if he wasn't interested in anything the shop had to offer, to make sure that if anybody else stopped at the same time, he'd notice. Nobody had.

It had got dark early, winter blanketing them

with a dusting of snow, reminding him that Christmas was only a week away.

London was full of gangs on mopeds these days, knifing people, robbing people and generally causing mayhem. They laughed at the law of course. They couldn't give a hoot about getting caught. What was the punishment anyway?

He was almost home now, safe once again. Not that he worried about himself. And he had badgered Carla to go to self-defence classes. She had laughed at him, especially when he had suggested she walk with some keys sticking out between her fingers.

He himself had been a boxer and still knew how to fight and he had tried to instill that sense into Carla. Hit him on the chin with the palm of your hand. Knee him in the balls. Poke him in the eyes.

She had suggested he hoped something would happen just so she could tell him how she'd taken the person down.

That had pissed him off. Her personal safety was nothing to laugh about, he had told her. There were nutters everywhere.

Even though they lived in a good part of London, people still came into the area where they lived, dangerous people. She had laughed at him, suggesting they get a big Rottweiler, but he had questioned the sanity of having a huge dog running about their house all day when they were at work.

Then Carla had told him the good news: she was pregnant. And the idea of getting a big dog had seemed more plausible. When the baby was born, they could grow up together. The dog wouldn't get jealous because he would see the baby as an equal.

Carla had promised him they would see. He had promised himself they would do more than see. He was getting a dog, and not a bouncy Lab either. He wanted one that would rip some bastard's throat out.

He climbed the steps to the house, looking down into the basement flat. There was a light on even though their tenant wasn't home. The man was young but still understood the importance of making sure a burglar thought somebody was in. He had taught the tenant that, and he had agreed. He was the best tenant they'd had, but he had gone back to Birmingham to spend time with his folks over Christmas.

He took his keys out and stopped dead in his tracks. It wasn't until he was standing right at the door that he'd noticed it wasn't closed all the way. He nudged it with his foot. It didn't creak. He'd told Carla that when it started creaking when the hinges dried out, he wasn't going to oil them. That would help them hear somebody coming in.

Again, she had laughed at that.

The door swung gently open. The lights were on in the hallway. He could hear the television on in the living room. He didn't call out. That would just alert somebody. He quietly stepped into the house and moved along the hall, knowing where to tread to avoid the squeaky floorboards. They had disagreed on that: she wanted the carpets lifted so they could have the floorboards nailed down properly to get rid of the squeaks, but he had told her – like the door! – that a stranger coming in wouldn't know where to step to avoid the noisy boards.

He peeked his head into the living room. Empty.

Maybe she had just gone out to speak to a neighbour. No, she knew he would go off his nut if she did that, leaving the front door open and unlocked. Wouldn't happen.

He looked up the stairs but didn't see any lights on.

He walked towards the back of the house, where the kitchen was. There were more lights on back there. They had talked about getting Chinese food in tonight, but maybe she had changed her mind. Her hormones were playing games with her, so maybe smoked sausage or something appealed more than lemon chicken. Or maybe she fancied peanut butter on pickles.

There was no smell of anything – weird or otherwise – being cooked. He clenched his fists, ready to literally go boxing with somebody, but when he stepped into the kitchen, his head swam for a few moments. His world tilted on its axis, and he leaned against the wall without realising he was doing it.

Then he screamed, but only in his head. He tried to shout out, and when he could eventually do it – it seemed like minutes later but was only seconds – he screamed out her name.

She couldn't hear him of course. Parts of her skull lay in the pool of blood that was spreading across the tiled floor.

'Carla! Carla! Can you hear me? Carla!'

Then he saw the pieces of her brain that had been ripped out by the weapon that had been used.

He called the operator and told the woman he needed an ambulance for his wife.

'Why? Because she has her brains scattered all over our fucking kitchen floor, that's why!' he screamed into the phone.

The detectives who turned up obviously thought he had killed his wife, despite him not having any blood on him. They questioned him for hours, but when they finally figured out the time of death, they learned he had been at work then, so they cut him some slack after that.

Despite the police conducting an extensive search, the killer was never caught.

He moved away after that. He had not only lost his wife but his little boy who had been growing inside her.

Would it have made a difference if they'd got the dog? Would his barking have scared the killer away so he moved on to somebody else? He would never know.

He moved far away, changing jobs and changing his whole appearance. He changed his name, not wanting people to associate him with the woman who had been murdered in her kitchen.

After he settled in, he had one more thing to do.

Join a therapy group.

And that was where he met the others.

TWENTY-NINE

Now

Craig pulled up in front of the house. It was in a nice part of Dunfermline, a semi-detached home that looked like it had been built in the 1970s.

'I wonder what he's going to say when we just knock on his door,' Bailey said.

'We're about to find out.'

'He's probably looking out from behind those net curtains,' Bailey said. 'So let's not keep him in suspense any longer.'

They got out and walked up the path and knocked on the front door. A gruff-looking man opened it. He had white hair that was sticking up on one side, as if he'd fallen asleep in a chair with his head leaning on one hand. He was unshaven, his stubble salt and pepper coloured. His eyes were deep and sharp under a furrowed brow. He was wearing a cardigan with a white vest under it, slippers instead of shoes, and trousers that looked like they hadn't been washed in...well, never. He seemed to be the very antithesis of his brother, the judge.

'What do you want?'

'Jeremy Keller?' Craig said.

'Who wants to know?'

'My name's James Craig. This is Tom Bailey.'

Keller sneered. 'So you're the one shacking up with my daughter.' He shook his head.

'Can we come in?' Bailey asked.

'Fuck me, you're not Scottish.'

'Ten out of ten. Is that a yes?'

'It's a no. Neither of you. And what you have to sell, I don't want to buy.'

'I wanted to talk to you about your brother,' Craig said.

'Which one?'

There's more than one? Craig thought but kept it to himself. 'Bill.'

'Willie? What's he done? Not much, considering he's in that home.'

'He's going downhill, your brother,' Bailey said.

'I know,' Keller replied.

'We just wanted to ask you a few questions about him,' Craig said.

'I don't have time and I'm not interested.'

'Not even for Annie's sake?' Craig said.

'Nope.'

'Listen, we're having a party for her tomorrow at the Pitreavie Golf Club. A birthday party. You're welcome to come along. Maybe mend some bridges.'

'We've had years to mend them and it didn't work out.'

'Is that why you were giving her a hard time on the phone today?' Craig said. 'She told me. But I think we should all sit down and have a drink. Bury the hatchet.'

'First of all, I'm a recovering alcoholic, and secondly, I haven't spoken to Annie in months. I don't know what she's blethering about.' Keller stepped back and closed his door on the two detectives.

'Christ, I forgot Annie told me her dad was an alkie,' Craig said as they walked back down the path to the car.

'Why would he lie about talking to Annie?' Bailey asked.

'I don't know.' But then Craig thought that maybe Jeremy Keller wasn't the one who had been lying.

THIRTY

Case # F – 4429636 – GC

Later on, when he thought about it back in the safety of his own home, he would think that if the bus driver had just waited instead of closing the doors and driving off, he might not have been driving his car at three o'clock in the early hours of a Saturday morning, wondering if he was going to be planning a funeral later that day.

The traffic was light, and the most dangerous thing about was young men in white t-shirts singing and dancing in the street, waving beer bottles and shouting at the top of their lungs.

One of them was still out there, brandishing a

knife – or maybe he'd thrown it away, or had taken it home to Mummy's house, where he paid digs and went out whenever he felt like it, while Mummy slaved in the house, washing his dirty underwear and the white t-shirts he wore when he went up to town on a Friday night, knife in pocket in case he got any 'agro'. *Bastard.*

He parked in the car park of Kirkcaldy's Victoria Hospital and rushed through to the A&E. The place was heaving, the result of a lot of booze being consumed and any inhibitions being thrown out the window. The drink suddenly made boxers out of men whose brain took every little thing said to heart and found that the only way to save face was to have a punch-up. Or stab somebody.

He went to the reception desk and explained who he was here to see, and was shown through to one of the little rooms where they told relatives and friends what was going on.

He heard the words like they were being spoken down a long funnel as his head reeled. Stabbing. Blood loss. Surgery. Not out of the woods.

He was asked if he understood and he nodded, but he didn't really understand. How could he? The love of his life was going to die. He could feel it. He didn't want to think like this, but there was nothing else for it. He was going to be on his own now, and he would never feel love again.

But the surgery was a success and time began to heal. He hadn't lost his love. And he would make sure nothing like this ever happened again.

But something changed. Fear took hold of his love. A fear that was deep-rooted. So he made the decision that they would co-habit before getting married.

First, though, there was one thing they would have to do. They would have to join group therapy.

And that was where they met the others.

THIRTY-ONE

Eve Craig was still reeling from what she had seen at her house in Dalgety Bay. Well, it wasn't *her* house anymore. It was technically his. But standing outside of it, kissing another woman...Had their twenty-five years of marriage been a lie? Had their feelings for each other just been skirting the surface? She wondered if her not being able to have her own children had affected him more than he had let on.

She wanted to be near her son, to be able to speak to him whenever she wanted to. The hospital wasn't like a prison. The people in there weren't there because they knew what they had done on the outside. They were there because they had committed crimes and weren't responsible for their actions.

She loved Jimmy and if truth be told, would never stop loving him, but they couldn't be together anymore. Their arguments had got worse, to the point where they couldn't have a civil conversation with each other.

That was why she was living alone in a small flat in a country town where nothing ever happened. But she was five minutes away from her little boy. Not so little anymore, but he'd always be her little Honeyman.

Of course, right now she wasn't entirely on her own.

'A glass of wine for the lady,' Chris Ward said, coming into her living room with two glasses and sitting down beside her on the couch, handing her a glass.

He clinked glasses with her. 'Cheers,' he said.

'Here's to us,' Eve said and smiled at him.

'To us. To our future together.'

They drank, then he leaned over and kissed her, slowly at first, then more passionately.

Then his phone rang.

He pulled away from her. 'Sorry, I need to see who this is. It might be the hospital.'

'That's okay. I know you're on call.' She smiled at

him as he got up from the couch and walked through to the kitchen.

'Hello,' he said, feeling his adrenaline kick in when he saw the number. It was for a disposable phone, but he knew it. The caller had called him on it before.

He closed the kitchen door softly as Eve put the TV on.

'It's time. Things are falling apart here. We've been dealing with it, but it's time to put it in high gear. You know what to do next.'

Ward looked round to make sure Eve wasn't standing there. 'That's fine, Doctor. I'll make sure he's taken care of,' he said in a loudish voice. Then in a whisper: 'Leave it with me. It'll get done.'

'Good man. Speak to you later.'

Ward hung up and walked back through to the living room.

'Everything alright?' she asked him.

'Yes. One of the men is getting a bit antsy. I have to go over tomorrow and have a session with him. I want them holding off on giving him more medication, and hopefully me talking to him will calm him down a bit.'

She smiled. 'Come and sit back down. I need you to put your arms around me right now.'

He smiled and sat down beside her. Then he started undressing her.

THIRTY-TWO

'Are you excited?' Craig asked Annie as she drank coffee in front of the TV.

'About what?' she said.

'Oh, I don't know, being with the most handsome guy on the planet.'

'Meh.' She held her hand out and rocked it back and forth. 'I am excited about the party tonight, though.'

'Teaser. But I'm looking forward to having everybody there too.' He drank some of his coffee, and then his phone rang. 'Hello?'

'Jimmy, it's Harry McNeil.'

'Hey, Harry, how's it going?'

'We got an ID on the victim from the cemetery. Len Croft. He lived in Kirkcaldy but worked in

Edinburgh. He went missing four years ago. They managed to get a partial print off a finger, and his name was in the database.'

'Don't tell me; he also had a record.'

'Attempted assault on a woman in a park. He walked free as there was nothing to connect him.'

'Jesus. Thanks for letting me know, Harry. If you email his details, I'll have one of my team go and talk with any relatives.'

'Thanks, Jimmy. See you tonight.'

Craig put the phone down and turned to Annie. 'That was Harry McNeil. They got an ID on the body they found in the cemetery. He's from Kirkcaldy, and he walked free from court after being charged with attempted assault on a woman.'

'Christ. Was my uncle the judge in the case?' Annie said.

Craig looked through the papers on the table and found Croft's name. 'Yes, he was.'

'Jesus Christ. What the hell is happening?'

'Listen, I don't have any proof, but I think your uncle was involved in something, and I don't think he was working alone.'

'What do you mean?' Annie said.

'I think when people walked free and weren't

punished, he and some others punished them. He's in the home right now, so it's not him doing it.'

'How do you know he's working with somebody else?'

'Because of what happened to Roger Hammond.'

'Jesus, Jimmy, that's a stretch.'

'Not when you're in my shoes.'

Annie shook her head and stood up and walked over to the window to look out over the sea. 'I can't believe my uncle would be like this. He was always an upstanding man. And his son was a judge too.'

'Was? I thought he still is?'

'Martin just retired. He's going to live in Spain.'

'Must be nice. He's only in his fifties, isn't he?'

'Yes,' she replied, turning to face him. 'He worked hard, though. He met a new girl, and they seem to be hitting it off.'

'I hope it works out for him.'

'You haven't met Martin, have you?' Annie said.

'I met him yesterday when we were in seeing Bill. He came in just as we were leaving.'

'He's nice, don't you think?'

'He seemed okay.'

'He and Michelle are hitting it off.'

'Michelle, the nurse at the home?' Craig asked.

'No, the woman he's seeing. I don't know who

she is. I think he would have said if it was Michelle from the home, don't you think?'

Not if he was trying to hide something. 'I don't know.' He moved closer to her. 'Listen, there's something I wanted to talk to you about.'

'Oh God, are you breaking up with me?'

'What? No, nothing like that. It's just that after you told me that you were arguing with your dad on the phone yesterday, I thought about it, and I don't want you to live the rest of your life with any regrets.'

'Such as not talking to my father again?'

'Yes. So Tom and I went to see him.'

Annie looked at him in silence.

'Say something,' he said. He wasn't expecting her to throw herself at him, but telling him that was wonderful would be appreciated.

'You did what?'

Craig hadn't seen this face on her before, but he had seen it on Eve, when he had somehow crossed the line.

'I was just trying to help.'

'Help? Help? What the fuck have you done? My father and I are estranged and that's the way I wanted it to be. How could you be so fucking stupid?'

'I just thought, after you were arguing yesterday –'

'I lied. I wasn't arguing with him. I wasn't even *talking* to him. Somebody sent me a text warning me off. *Drop it. Last warning.*'

'Why didn't you tell me?'

'I didn't want you to worry. Somebody doesn't want me to keep talking to my uncle. But now you've gone and fucked things with my father. Jesus, Jimmy. You don't know what you've done.'

She started to walk out of the living room.

'Can't we just talk about it?'

'What's there to talk about? The damage is done.' She looked at her watch. 'I have a PM to do.'

He watched her walk out of his living room. He wanted to go and talk to Bailey.

THIRTY-THREE

Annie was so mad at Craig that she could have spat nails. How dare he do that to her! What was he thinking? Being a do-gooder, that's what. And dragging Tom Bailey along with him! Although she wasn't mad at Bailey. No, this was firmly on Craig's shoulders.

She pulled into the small car park at the back of the hospital, where the entrance to the mortuary receiving area was. She unlocked the door and walked along to her office. She couldn't help feeling her life was falling apart, just when she was getting it back on track.

She went into her office, turned the lights on, sat down in her chair and looked at the clock. The boys wouldn't be here for a little while yet. She wished they were here now so they could get started, but they were on call, and she'd only let them know a little while ago that she wanted to start the postmortem.

Her thoughts turned to her father and the fight she'd had with him, and the decision that would shape her whole future.

'You want to be a what?' Jeremy Keller said to his daughter. 'Over my dead body.'

'Why? I'm old enough to make my own decisions. Mum would have approved of me being a solicitor.'

'Don't you bring your fucking mother into this!' Keller was drunk again, which was the norm for him. He'd started early this evening, skipping dinner and going straight for the whisky. *I want to get drunk faster tonight and you can do that on an empty stomach,* he had told her.

Now he was standing in front of her, swaying, his breath smelling sour, his body smelling even worse. When was the last time he'd showered?

Annie doubted that he'd showered since her mother's funeral a week ago.

'You do what you want with your life, but I'm going to do what I want with mine.'

'No, you're fucking not.' He reached out to grab her arm, but she dodged him. He overbalanced and fell onto the living room carpet. But as with drunks the world over, he didn't feel it. He might do in the morning, but right now, he bounced back onto his feet.

'You were just a bairn when I was on the picket lines. Fighting with the police. Trying to stop a mad woman down south from closing our pits. So you didn't see the beatings we got. We were in fights with the uniforms. Those were tough days, but you were only five years old, so what would you know? No matter how hard times got, we still put food on the table. You don't know how many times I came home to your mother bruised and battered, and for what? Nothing in the end. The corruption started way back then. Politicians getting their pockets lined. All the while fucking us over. And now you want to have a job where you'll be working with them all the time! Jesus Christ. Think about it, Annie. Just think about it.'

And she had. She researched what had happened back in the days when a power-tripping female politician got her own way.

It was after that that she decided to go into medicine. But the rot had set into her relationship with her father. There were times when she would be studying, and then years later, crying out for sleep and getting none, she hated her father the most.

But she had become a doctor, then a pathologist, and she loved her work. That didn't mean she wanted to be in her father's company, though.

Or did she? Was it time to mend bridges?

She took her phone out and stared at it, wanting to call her father, but she couldn't bring herself to do it.

But then, she didn't have to call him. He was calling her.

'Dad?'

'Listen, I've been thinking about things ever since your boyfriend came round to see me yesterday. Life's too short to hold grudges. We need to talk.'

'Dad...I don't think I'm ready to talk. Let me just have time to think about it.'

'No, pumpkin, we need to talk about it now.

You've been seeing Bill for a while now, and his dementia has been getting worse. I went in to see him the other day, and that stuff he's talking about? Albert Fish?'

'What do you mean, dangerous?'

'The things he's done. It would make your skin crawl. But it's ending now. I got a call in the wee hours. Bill died last night.'

'Oh Jesus, no! Please, no!' she shouted.

'He did some bad things, but it was all in the name of good. He took care of the man who hurt your mum. They made him disappear. I knew about it, and was happy to go along with it, but they're dangerous. Now that Bill has been talking, they'll want to distance themselves from him.'

'Dad, you're not making sense. Who are *they*?'

'I can't tell you. I don't want you to be in danger. Any more than you are now. If they think you don't know about them, then they'll leave us alone.'

Tears were running down Annie's cheeks now. 'You're going to be alright now, Dad, aren't you?'

'I hope so.'

Annie heard the receiving door opening through by the PM suite. *It must be the boys,* she thought. She didn't really want them to see her like this, but she couldn't end the call just to tidy herself up. She wanted to know her father would be alright.

'Dad, I'll call Jimmy. Get him to come and see you.'

There was silence for a moment, then her father came back on the line.

'Too late,' he said. Then the line went dead.

THIRTY-FOUR

Craig was over at Annie's house in Dunfermline, having a coffee with Bailey and Biggie.

'What are you thinking here, lad?' Bailey asked Craig. 'That Bill Keller was involved in killing people?'

'I'm not sure if he soiled his hands, but yes, I think he was involved. Something was niggling away at me last night, and I just couldn't reach it, but this morning, when I was in my bathroom shaving, it came to me. Bill said that the killer is in the home, the man he calls Albert Fish – it's Bill himself.'

'Jesus,' Biggie asked.

'Bill said that the killer has a little scar above his lip. I didn't think any more of it, reckoning he was imagining things. Then I was standing looking at myself in the mirror as I shaved, and I remembered that *Bill* has a little scar above his lip. He's been looking at himself.'

'Jesus,' Bailey said.

'It doesn't prove anything,' Craig said, 'but I do think he was involved in those men dying.'

Craig's phone rang. He looked at the screen and saw Annie's name. He was about to answer, but remembered one time when he and Eve had fought and she had called him to keep the fight going. This could go either way.

He answered it.

'Jimmy? My uncle Bill died last night.'

'What? Oh Jesus.'

'But listen, my dad called me and he's in trouble. Somebody's in his house. Can you go there? Please, Jimmy. I'm sorry about earlier.'

'I'll go right now. I'm in your house with Tom and Biggie.'

'I'll meet you there. I'll leave the mortuary right now.'

'Annie, knowing you, you'll get there before I do. Do not go inside. You wait outside.'

'Okay.'

She disconnected the call and Craig jumped up.

Bailey and Biggie were already on their feet, grabbing their jackets.

'Bill died last night. When we left, I saw some people enter his room and close the door. I'll tell you on the way.'

'We're going to the home?'

'No, Tom. Annie thinks her dad is in trouble and asked us to go to his place. Actually, just me, but I figured you would want to come.'

'Let's go. Biggie, you have my permission to get that jalopy going like stink.'

THIRTY-FIVE

Annie was in a panic. She knew she had to get to her dad. Somebody was with him at the house, and she was sure now that her uncle's death hadn't been from natural causes.

But like Craig, something was nagging at her. The number she'd received the text from. She had seen it before.

She had been standing in the corridor when she called Craig, but now she went back into her office. There was a piece of paper on her desk somewhere. There was so much clutter on her desk. Organised chaos, she called it. Little knickknacks she had picked up when she had been on holiday. Usually, she picked up a fridge magnet, but on occasion, she had picked up other things. They had reminded her of when she had gone on holiday with her ex-husband, Monty, and she had thrown a lot of that stuff out, but she'd kept some of it just because she liked it.

She knew she should be better organised, but life got in the way. Every few months she had a purge, and little sticky notes got thrown away, papers shredded; once, she had even found a foosty chocolate bar wrapper.

Today, though, she was looking for a piece of paper with a phone number on it.

Then she remembered: during one such purge, she had decided to stick the phone numbers on a magnetic board in the PM suite. They would be handy right there.

She left her office and went through the doors into the main area. She was expecting to see the boys, or even one of them, but it was eerily quiet. Maybe one of them had opened the garage door to... do what?

There was nobody there. Had they gone into the PM suite without popping along to her office to see if she was in?

She went into the suite where the PMs were done, all shiny steel tables and instruments and an antiseptic smell. A familiar smell to her. It made her feel comfortable, made her feel that she had made the right decision in becoming a doctor. If working in law made you feel like killing people who walked out of court free, then she had definitely chosen the right career.

She walked over to the magnetic board where pieces of paper were stuck on. Phone numbers.

And she saw it there. The number from the text. And the fear made the skin on her neck crawl.

When she turned round, he was right there, not two feet from her. He had taken his shoes off and she hadn't heard him coming. It was his number.

'Hello, Annie,' he said.

THIRTY-SIX

The front door was open. Not ajar, but open.

'Jeremy?' Craig said, stepping in, Bailey and Biggie close behind him.

Bailey looked at the younger detective. 'You've got better knees than me. Use them to run up the stairs and see if there's any bastard up there. If there is, scream like a young lass, like you always do, and we'll come up and give the bastard a good belting.'

Biggie ignored him and ran up the stairs as Craig led the way into the living room.

It looked like the place had been turned upside down.

'Maybe he decided to tackle whoever came in after him,' Bailey said.

'Looks like he put up a good fight.' Craig left the

room and went through to the kitchen, and they heard Biggie thumping down the stairs.

'Nothing disturbed upstairs.'

'The living room looks like yours on a good day,' Bailey said.

'Me mam will be pleased to hear that.'

Bailey pointed his finger at Biggie. 'Don't go rocking the boat with me and your mam. She makes me a bloody good bacon sarnie.'

Craig came back out of the kitchen. 'It looks like whoever was here took Keller, or maybe he managed to escape. What's your gut say about this, Tom?'

'If he's around Bill's age, then I shouldn't think he did any running. I would say somebody took him out of here.'

They heard somebody knocking on the front door. Craig marched up the hallway with the others behind him. He opened the door and saw an old woman standing there, rubbing her hands together.

'Can I help you?' Craig asked. 'I'm DCI Craig.'

'I was just wondering if Jeremy is okay. Have you heard?'

'Did you see anything?' Bailey asked from behind Craig.

'His friend took him out of here a wee while ago. About an hour ago, something like that.'

'Can you describe his friend?' Craig asked.

'Big fella. He looked ordinary. I was more looking at Jeremy, who needed to be helped along the path. The man said Jeremy had fallen and he was taking him to the Victoria.'

'What kind of car did he have?' Bailey asked.

'Oh, he didn't have a car, son.'

THIRTY-SEVEN

Biggie drove like he was in a video game and every other car on the road didn't exist. Craig called DSup Baker, and the boss told him he would make the phone calls and meet him over there with Dan and Isla.

Craig knew Dan would be a rock, but Isla would lose it. He had tried calling Annie, but her phone was switched off, and she never switched her phone off when she was in the mortuary, not after what had happened a few weeks ago.

Baker said he would blue-light a patrol to the mortuary to see if she was there.

Five minutes later, Craig got a call back.

'She's not in the mortuary, Jimmy. There was already a patrol in the hospital, and they went and

WHISPERS OF GUILT

looked. There's no sign of a disturbance. I got them to open the fridge drawers, and the two assistants had just arrived and they said the place was empty when they got there, despite Annie calling them and asking them to come in and help with a PM. They helped search the drawers, but Annie wasn't in any of them. Her car is still parked outside. I had the hospital make a call to see if anybody saw her, but she would have her phone on her. Nobody's seen her.'

'Thanks, boss.'

'I'll be right there. Patrols have been dispatched, but I told them to wait.'

'Thanks. We won't be long. Five minutes.'

The business was in an industrial park just outside Kelty. Biggie slowed down as they entered through the gates. It was well maintained, with a decent car park.

'Slow it down, Biggie, and don't slam the doors when we get out,' Craig said.

Biggie nodded and pulled in beside a van. He turned the engine off and they all got out, making as little noise as possible. This was a country sound, and not even the traffic on the motorway in the distance could be heard.

There were some other cars parked near the back

door. Craig and the others approached the door, and it wasn't locked. They went inside and heard voices. Craig took out his phone and shot off a text to Baker: *Now*.

He knew they should wait, but he couldn't. Time was running out.

They were in a receiving area, not huge but big enough. Another door led through to the main area, where the work was done.

'Shock and awe, lad,' Bailey said, leading the way. The inner door was booted, and the three men were in.

A group of people were standing around. Four of them. Two people were sitting on chairs. Annie and her father. One of the group grabbed Annie.

'Why don't you come in?' the leader said. 'There's plenty of room for everyone.'

THIRTY-EIGHT

Chris Ward was making his rounds. There were no sessions on a Saturday, but sometimes the guests would act up, and they could either talk to him or have their medication increased.

He walked with an orderly along the corridor in one of the wings. 'Let's see how this young fella is doing.'

The orderly nodded and unlocked the door. Ward had just been to see another young man and had slipped him a little something that would make him sick.

One of the other orderlies ran towards that man's room. 'Oh Christ, that's him being sick again. He's been sick all week.'

I know he has, Ward wanted to say. *I'm the one who's been making him sick.*

'Go and help,' Ward said to the orderly who was with him. 'Joe will be alright. He's had his medication early this morning?'

'Yes, sir.'

'Go. I'll be fine.'

The orderly ran along the corridor, and Ward stepped into the room. 'Joe. Nice to see you. How have you been?'

Joe had an alter ego, but that one didn't seem to have got out of bed yet. Joe looked at him and nodded. 'Fine.' His voice was barely a whisper. The meds were taking effect.

'You've been good recently. I like it when you're good. I hate it when you're bad. You remember when you were bad?'

Joe stared at him, drool starting its descent down from the corner of his mouth. Ward hated increasing the dosage of his meds, but for what he was about to do, he needed Joe compliant.

'I have something for you, something that will make you sleep,' Ward said. 'But first, let me ask you something. When you were killing women in London, taking a hammer to them?'

He took out the syringe.

'Do you remember a young woman who you killed in her kitchen?'

Took the cap off.

'Her name was Joanne Sowerby. She was pregnant. She was my wife.'

He put the needle into Joe's arm.

'They found out much later that it was you. And now look where you are: in a cushy psychiatric hospital instead of in prison like a man.'

He pressed the plunger.

'The group took me under their wing. Told me how I could get back at you.'

Ward took the needle out and put the cap back on and stuck the syringe in his pocket. Then he laid Joe down on his bed.

A few moments later, the orderly came back.

'Joe's sleeping now. His meds have kicked in. Just lock the door and check on him later. Probably a few hours.'

'Right you are, sir.'

'How's the patient down there?' Ward asked.

'We gave him some anti-nausea meds. He'll be fine in a little while.'

Ward looked at his watch. 'Right, I'd better be off. I have a committee meeting to go to. And on a Saturday too. Just my luck.' He patted the orderly on the arm. 'See you later.'

Ward walked out of the hospital. Of course, he wouldn't see the orderly later, or ever again.

He would travel down to London and use the fake passport to fly out of Heathrow and on to New York. Hopefully, he'd be winging his way over the Atlantic by the time they went in to wake Joe.

He laughed at that.

THIRTY-NINE

'Well, well, the gang's all here,' Craig said. He looked at Martin Keller, who had a tight grip on Annie. The large room smelled dusty, maybe from the remnants in the furnace over to one side. 'Was it you who killed your father last night? Or was that somebody else?'

Michelle smiled at him. 'That was me. We couldn't risk him babbling anymore.'

Craig nodded.

Bailey stepped forward. 'You're Suzie Carr, I take it? Now calling yourself Michelle.'

'Shut up,' Garfield Clover said.

'It doesn't matter now, Garfield,' Michelle said. 'I don't care what he calls me. Eddie Hay died a violent death. I can die a happy woman knowing he died a lot more painfully than I will.'

Jackson Clover was sitting over by the coffin he'd brought Annie here in. 'I don't feel good at all.' He leaned to one side and vomited.

Jeremy Keller was sitting near the other coffins, his mouth bleeding where he'd been punched. His hands were tied behind his back.

Annie was struggling. 'Let me go, you bastard,' she said.

'Let her go, Martin,' Michelle said.

'I don't think so,' Martin answered. Then he suddenly pushed Annie away from him and grabbed his chest. He fell to his knees and then onto his face.

The furnace flames were eager to get some flesh to eat, but they suddenly died until they were extinguished.

Michelle turned to Craig. 'Is that your colleagues outside turning off the gas?'

'I assume so.'

Garfield looked at Annie. 'I'm sorry about all of this. But Michelle and I want to leave here. You're going to help us leave.' He looked at his brother, who was now lying prone on the floor. 'Sorry to you too, Jackson, but it has to be this way. Five of us on the run was always going to look stupid.'

Craig counted heads again, confused: Martin Keller, Garfield and Jackson Clover, Michelle – four. Who was number five?

Annie stood beside her father, looking at the others. Garfield grabbed her by the arm. She tried to shake him off, but he was too big and strong.

'Five?' Bailey asked. 'There's only four of you here. Who's number five?'

'Doesn't matter now,' Michelle said.

'Let's take this snooping cow and get out of here,' Garfield said.

'Didn't you hear Craig? His colleagues are outside. They're not going to let you leave. Or me.'

'I want to give it a bloody good try. That's what we planned, Michelle.'

'That's what *you* planned, Garfield. You and Martin and your brother. You all planned to burn those two and then we would all leave. But Annie is too smart for that. She would let Craig know somehow. Or if not, he'd figure it out. He's a good detective. I didn't see us getting away.'

Garfield's eyes went wide, and then he started making a choking noise, letting go of Annie's arm before falling face down onto the concrete floor.

Michelle looked at Annie. 'You were never in any danger. You or your dad. I just went along with their plan so I could get you all here in one place. If Craig here hadn't turned up, I would have called him to come and get you.'

She nodded to the coffee cups on a table that had come from a coffee shop. She smiled.

'I was the one who stopped for the coffees. I was the one who laced them. Muscle relaxant. It stops the heart. But just for good measure, a little something to make them sick at the same time. A little extra sugar covered the taste.'

'You're going to take the fall for them all?' Biggie said.

Michelle looked at him. 'You'll learn more as the years go on.' She looked at Craig. 'Tell him.'

'You spiked your own coffee, just with not quite the same dosage as the others. So you could tell us about what you did.' Craig brought out his phone and started recording.

Michelle started wheezing a bit, her lungs struggling now. 'After Martin was attacked, they were convinced it was Stephen Colby. When he got off, Bill was furious. So he and Martin killed a prostitute, cut her ear off and burned her in there.' She nodded to the furnace. 'They put the ear and some clothes in Colby's attic. The family members of the missing women didn't know what clothes they had been wearing. The ear and the clothes were enough to get Colby convicted. He didn't kill anybody.'

'What about those two?' Bailey said, nodding to the brothers.

'Garfield got a kicking from a couple of thugs. They walked. Garfield and Jackson joined the therapy group where Martin, Bill and I met. They were groomed so they could join us and get revenge. We helped them kill Len Croft, and we dumped him in the cemetery in Warriston to throw the police off our scent. No one found him. We went back and cut back the long grass around him so he would be found – eventually – by the club of volunteers who go there. Same with that bastard Hay. We wanted him found. Those were the only two we'd hid. Others we put in the furnace. Then when you looked into it, and talked to Bill, which we were sure you would, he would get the blame as he was the judge who presided over their cases, and he was talking about a killer being in the home. We hoped you would put two and two together. But he started talking to Annie and was having lucid moments. He was giving too much away. He had to be silenced. Which he was, last night.

'I promise you, I would never have let them hurt Annie or her dad.' Michelle looked at Annie, her breathing slowing down. 'As I said, I just had to let Jackson bring you here so I could finish this.'

'Was there supposed to be somebody else here, Michelle?' Craig said, walking towards her. He stopped and looked her in the eye. 'Please tell me.'

Her breath was rasping now. 'Another...member. I don't know...much about him. He's...a doctor. Not... in Fife. His wife...beaten...to death...hammer...' Michelle fell face down onto the floor.

Bailey called Mark Baker. 'You can come in. No rush. They're all dead.'

The doors burst open with a firearms team and Mark Baker rushed in anyway, with other uniforms behind him.

Annie untied her father's hands from behind his back and got him to his feet. She started crying and held on to him. He held her and tears rolled down his face.

When she turned around, she saw Craig in a corner. He'd turned his phone's recorder off, and he was talking into the phone now. Then he hung up. She let go of her father and walked over to Craig.

'Is everything okay?'

Craig shook his head. 'Michelle spoke about a doctor whose wife was murdered by a hammer killer. That's Joe.'

Annie sucked in a breath and put a hand over her mouth. 'Oh God, Jimmy.'

'I called Eve to get her to talk to the doctor she's friendly with. See if he knows if Joe is okay.'

Annie held him.

'What the hell happened here?' Baker asked Bailey.

'Michelle knew it was over and poisoned the others, and took a slightly lower dose for herself to make sure the others died first. Murder-suicide. Those bastards were killing people. Some they hid, but others...' Bailey nodded to the furnace.

'Jesus. I wonder if any of the victims went in alive?'

'We'll never know now.'

Craig's phone rang. Eve was hysterical. She didn't need to speak any words.

FORTY

'It doesn't seem like it's been a month,' Annie said as they walked along the riverbank in Langholm, in the Scottish Borders.

'Christ, it took a long time for the procurator fiscal to release his body,' Craig said.

'There was a lot to sort out, to be fair.'

'I know.'

The water was low, so they could walk on the stones that would be covered by the river later, when winter came and the rains swelled the river. Annie picked up a flat stone and skimmed it across. Finn jumped in and then stopped, looking at where the stone had gone.

'This is hard, Annie. On the one hand, he was my son, but on the other hand, he killed people.'

'Just focus on the good times you had with him. That will ease the pain.'

He nodded. He was carrying the urn under one arm. 'My grandfather used to come here and spend the summers with his aunt, uncle and cousins. He loved it. So did my dad. We scattered my grandfather's ashes at this very spot.'

Craig unscrewed the cap and took it off. He stepped forward, getting closer to the river, and slowly emptied what remained of Joe into the gently rushing water. He stood and quietly cried for a few moments, then took a hanky out of his pocket and dried his eyes as Annie came over and put an arm around his waist. Finn came up and nudged his head against Craig's leg.

'Are you going to look for...you know...?' she asked Craig.

'Not personally. The man who killed him lost his wife to Joe. He came home one night and found his wife dead on the kitchen floor. She was pregnant. The authorities are looking for him, but he's well gone now. I doubt we'll ever find him.'

'Eve must feel so bad, being duped by him.'

'She isn't saying anything to me. She didn't want any part of this today.'

Craig stood looking at the grey powder slowly

being taken away by the river. When he could see no more of it, they turned and walked back up to the pathway above.

AFTERWORD

I would like to thank some people for making this job easier - Jacqueline Beard, who is a treasure. Lisa McDonald and her husband Gary Menzies for their continued support. To my daughters. My wife too. And my dogs, Bear and Bella, who never get bored coming down to the office with me.

And a huge thanks to you, the reader, for coming along for the ride.

I recently had my Frank Miller short story - Old School - re-edited and republished it as many of you asked where they could get a copy. new cover too! More short stories coming.

If anybody wants to get in touch, please feel free to contact me through my website, www.johncarsonau

thor.com I'll get around to replying to each and every one. Just bear with me.

John

ABOUT THE AUTHOR

John Carson is originally from Edinburgh, Scotland, but now lives with his wife and family in New York State. And two dogs. And four cats.

www.johncarsonauthor.com

Printed in Great Britain
by Amazon